The Door to Trilesk

Shannon Holly

Painite Publishing

Cover by Gombar Cover Design
Formatting by Polgarus Studio

ISBN: 979-8-218-36213-3

Published by Painite Publishing
Amherst, Ohio, USA

Dedicated to the dreamers, the ones who get lost in daydreams or in the clouds. The ones who look at every sunset, and moon and flower with awe and appreciation. Never lose that magic.

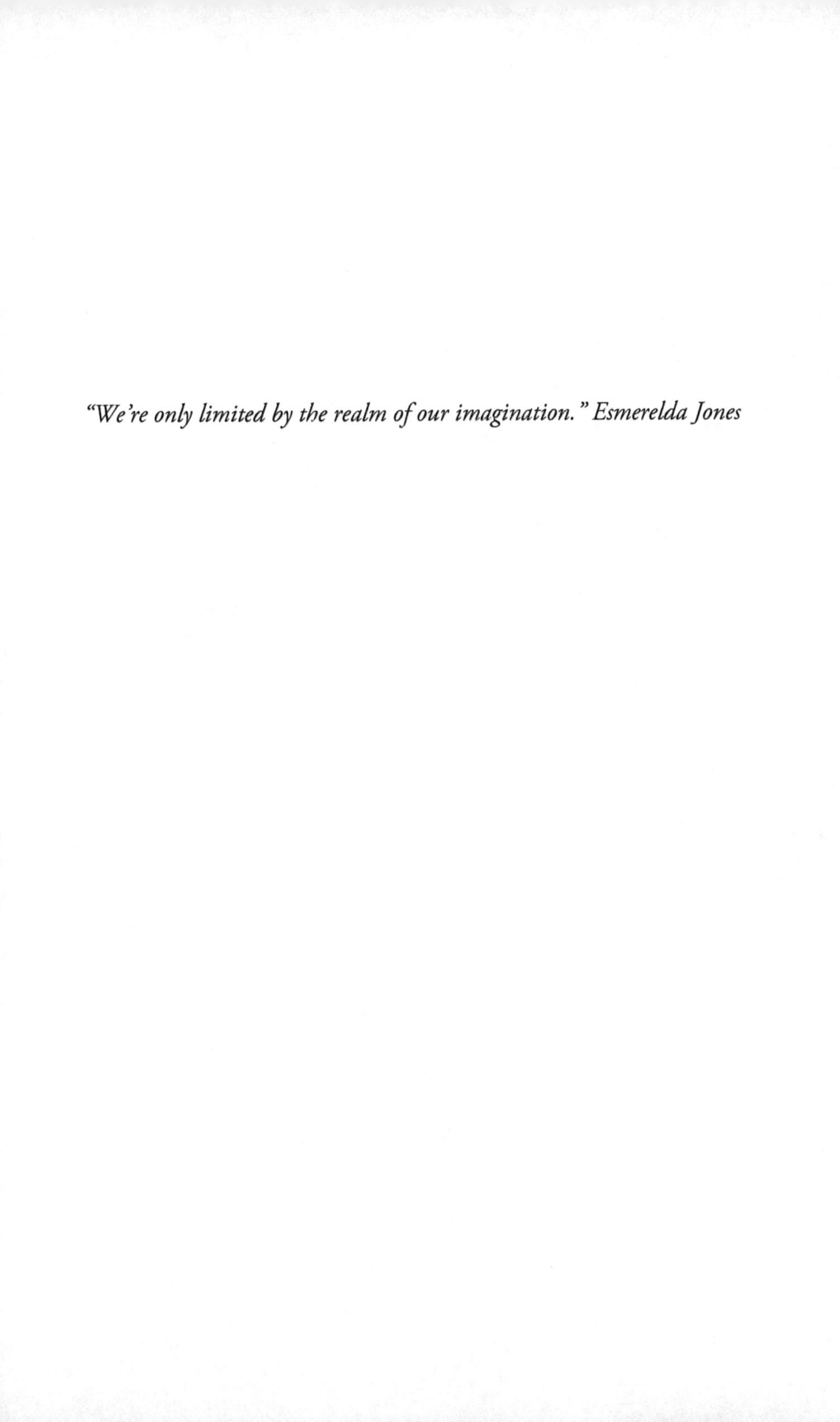

"We're only limited by the realm of our imagination." Esmerelda Jones

1) The House

Kate gripped the steering wheel with white knuckles as a single drop of sweat dripped down the middle of her rigid back. Her muscles tensed with the effort to contain the panic that had driven her here: to her estranged, missing, aunt's house. Like a wild beast it reared up and beat against her breast. *Now Now Now.* She dropped her forehead onto the steering wheel and groaned. None of this made sense. What was she even doing here? If her mom found out where she was… Well Kate knew how badly that would end.

After all, what did she care what her mom did with it? It was just a house. Kate scoffed at the thought. Yeah. *Just* a house that had been in her mom's family for centuries. *Just* a house her mom and aunt had grown up in. *Just* a house Kate had never been allowed near, except for one summer years ago. Kate exhaled sharply. *Just* a house she had no memory of. Not a single one. So if her mom wanted to get rid of it, it shouldn't matter to her. Yet somehow it did. Somehow this place pulled her back to it with every fiber of her being, ever since she discovered her mom's plans. Somehow, something mattered enough to drive her here knowing the trouble it would cause if she was found out. She sighed again. There was still time to go home. She could start the car and turn it around, try to ignore the frantic foreboding, but she knew she couldn't. She needed to see what was calling her back.

Kate gathered her courage, opened the door, and stepped out. She looked up and took in the house and yard that exuded her aunt's energy: from the house's paint color—dark purple fading into a lighter purple on top—to the metal art sculptures and concrete faces her aunt made that were scattered throughout the lush flower garden and left no room for mere grass, to the meandering stone path that ended under the giant canopy of an ancient oak tree. At least she thought it was an oak; she had really never seen an oak, or any tree, that big. The massive tree branches brushed the sky, and Kate swore the tree whispered as the leaves rustled.

Smells and colors exploded across the lush garden, and birds launched through the foliage, sweet trills of happiness bursting from their beaks. In fact, everywhere twenty-year-old Kate looked, plants and animals alike seemed, well, happy. But that was impossible, wasn't it? Tiny voices everywhere seemed to welcome her home. Insects played their wings like cellos, hummingbirds darted to and fro, and other colorful birds Kate couldn't identify added to the music with their warbles. A cloud of butterfly wings flitted like soft kisses over her cheeks. *Home*, her heart sang. *Home*, the plants rustled with the wind. *Home*, rejoiced the animals like a page torn from a child's storybook.

Kate felt wetness on her cheeks and swiped away tears that had fallen unnoticed as her body recognized the longing, well before her head acknowledged that she had missed this place something fierce. Kate blew out a breath and tried to shake the spell. She spotted a trio of concrete frogs by the front porch that seemed almost familiar and made her way over. Instinctively she pushed the middle frog's head down. Its mouth sprang open, and a tongue unfurled to reveal an intricate, old, tarnished brass key. Surprised and half expecting it to be wet, Kate grabbed the key and somehow knew it would fit the front door lock. Such a small thing really, yet the thought of another family touching it, using it to get into her aunt's house filled her with such sorrow. She shook her head to dispel the thoughts and walked up to the front door. She inserted the key and felt the tumblers turn and pushed the door inward. Everything was eerily still, as if the house was holding its breath, waiting for. . . . For what, exactly? Her glorious return? More likely the stillness was because no one had lived here since her aunt disappeared a year ago. Kate snorted at the ridiculousness and stepped across the threshold. She closed the door and marveled as the sun splashed colors over the carpet through the colored glass mural in the door that depicted a mermaid in the water. The craftsmanship was extraordinary, down to the small details that made it appear as if the mermaid were actually swimming.

Kate glanced over the rest of the front room and guessed it was a parlor. It seemed all old houses had parlors. This particular one contained sofas and chairs set up for conversations and entertaining with lots of natural light coming from all the windows. Pieces from her aunt's travels filled the room, each with a unique story to tell of how and where it had been acquired.

A framed picture caught Kate's eye and she wandered over and picked it up. The camera had caught a much younger Esmerelda, mid-laugh, looking directly into the lens. She looked so vivacious. Her hands trembled as she set the picture down. The knowledge that she would never be able to ask her aunt what she was laughing about or who took the picture or why the memory was so important that her aunt had the picture framed washed over her. Her aunt had been such a unique person, never afraid to be her true self, confident and happy with who she was. Kate looked forward to her aunt's visits on birthdays and holidays when she could bask in that energy, so different from her mom's, for at least a few hours. As the years went by, she saw less and less of her as her aunt's travels took her away more and more. Kate vividly remembered the last time her aunt came to see her. It was two years ago on Kate's eighteenth birthday. She had been so wrapped up in her friends and becoming an adult she blew off all her aunt's attempts to talk to her. After all, at that point Kate barely knew her. Everything was fine until she caught her aunt looking at her with such sorrow that grief gripped Kate's heart so tight she could barely breathe. She moved to talk to her aunt privately but each time her mom appeared, making conversations difficult, until finally it was too late. Her aunt left and the feeling faded into the background, making Kate doubt the whole encounter. Questions gnawed at her, but Kate ignored them and turned her attention back to the room. She took a few steps towards the center of the room, intent on exploring the rest of the house, but stopped in her tracks as her aunt's presence wrapped around her like a warm hug. Gone was the stillness. Instead, it felt like her aunt just popped into the kitchen for a moment to make some of her homemade lavender iced tea. Lavender iced tea? Kate shook her head, confused. She'd never had lavender iced tea, yet she tasted the subtle flavors of mint and lavender on her tongue.

"A bit of tea time." Aunt Esmerelda marched into the room followed by an eight-year-old Kate. Her aunt carried a tray holding a large French press, stuffed with lavender and mint, steeping in hot water. Tall glasses clinked with ice, and a white plate laced with delicate blue flowers was piled high with Kate's favorite lemon cookies. They both wore explorer outfits complete with binoculars, boots, and hats, all smudged with dirt.

"The trick is to steep it for ten minutes. Not one minute more or less," her aunt stated as she set the tray down.

"Lavender's my favorite!" eight-year-old Kate quipped.

"What about hibiscus? You said that was your favorite yesterday."

"Well, it was my favorite yesterday. Today my favorite's lavender!"

"Lucky for us we have our own unlimited supply of lavender." Aunt Esmerelda tickled Kate's nose with the tiny purple flower. Past and

present Kate giggled, and Kate's eyes grew wide. She remembered this! She remembered all the iced teas they would make from her aunt's herb garden. Hibiscus, lavender, chocolate mint, orange thyme, along with exotic-sounding herbs with the most amazing flavors that made the best iced tea. How could she have forgotten that? She watched her younger self fling her little body into her aunt's arms in a fierce hug.

"I hope this never ends, Aunt Esme. I love you," little Kate whispered. She strained to hear her aunt's reply, but it was too soft. Their laughter trailed away like a puff of smoke as the vision faded. She stood rooted to the spot, willing it back.

A slow burn between her shoulder blades brought her back to the present and she stretched her neck down and turned her head to the side. How could she have forgotten this? What other memories were locked inside here? Kate let her feet lead her further inside the house, and ignored the flicker of fear at the thought of her mom finding out she was here. This was worth the tongue-lashing, or at least that's what she kept telling herself. It was one thing to think about it and quite another to experience it. Kate winced and pushed the thought away. It was only for one day and her mom would never find out.

Kate ventured down a hallway as it opened up through a large stone archway. She stopped as her eyes took in the room that opened before her. It was a solarium, like the ones you would see in the old movies, that was almost as large as the rest of the house. Glass panel walls soared above her to merge with a glass ceiling, each pane separated with black iron scrollwork that must have taken weeks, even months, to finish. The floors were inlaid with patterned cream, green, and gold tiles, placed to create the look of flowers sprinkled throughout the floor. Lush, tropical plants, both large and small, filled the space. Here and there cozy couches and chairs created bubbles of private oases, ripe for reading a good book, or just getting lost in one's own thoughts.

Kate's feet instinctively carried her along until they stopped in a corner of the room occupied by an empty easel that sat expectantly. A beige canvas lay underneath to protect the floors, an art piece unto itself with splashes and drops of overlying hues—vibrant reds, blues, and purples, soft pastels in pinks and lilacs, stark blacks and whites. Jars littered both surfaces of the two tables that flanked the easel; some were filled with brushes from finite to large house painter's type, others filled with what had been watered-down paint, now dried, cracked, and clinging to life on the sides of the jar. A stack of white canvases leaned against the wall. Forgotten and forlorn, this nook spoke to Kate about all the endless possibilities. Her fingers twitched, eager to grab a paintbrush and start creating. Joy followed by chagrin made Kate squirm. How had she not known her aunt was an artist? Had anyone else in her family painted? She sighed. She would probably never know. Her mom never talked about what little family they had, and if it had to do with art… forget it. Her mom never said anything that might encourage Kate's career choice.

An alarm halted Kate's thoughts and she swiped her phone to silence it, leaving a smear of sweat. It was almost time for her meeting with Morgan. Kate's hands trembled at the prospect. Morgan Lovejoy was the successful owner of an art gallery that hosted a ONO—One Night Only—Exhibit that drew collectors from around the world. Along with the top artists, Morgan would choose a lucky local artist to showcase at the event, and Kate desperately wanted to be the one chosen for the event.

She headed towards the front of the house and her stomach tightened in knots. This was the part she hated the most. Meeting face-to-face, letting some stranger judge her work, exposing her soul to wounds by the slightest frown, or offhand comments the other person never remembers but in turn scars. It was brutal. And talking about herself and her work? It made her feel like a child playing dress-up in oversized fancy clothes, not like the adult she had been for two years. She tried living by the adage "fake it till you make it," but sometimes faking that confidence grew heavy. When would she feel more like an adult? When would she feel powerful, confident, and fully herself? Not some pint-sized version who, to be honest, had no belief in herself right now.

A gentle breeze wrapped itself around Kate and followed her to the car. She opened the door but froze when she heard her name whispered in the wind. *Kate.* She shook her head and plopped into the car. Nerves were getting the better of her. It had been a crazy, emotional day, more so than she could have ever foreseen at the start of the day. She just needed to get through this meeting and then she could melt into a pajama puddle at home.

A few hours later her roommate and best friend pounced on Kate as she walked in the front door of their apartment.

"What happened? How'd it go? You haven't answered any of my texts! I mean, I know you're horrible at texting back, but I thought you would have made an exception for this! Tell me! Tell me everything! Was she amazed by your talent?" Maggie fired at Kate, barely giving her time to respond.

Kate shrugged her shoulders, letting her portfolio slide to the floor.

"She was not amazed. She said my pieces had promise but were missing something."

"What could possibly be missing from your work? It's incredible." Maggie asked with a frown.

"Authenticity." Kate turned to face her best friend. Her stomach clenched along with her teeth at the sting of rejection.

"What does that even mean? You paint fantasy, which does not denote authenticity."

"I don't know, Maggie. She absolutely refused to elaborate or explain it anymore. She said it was for me to discover. She did say that if I found my authentic inner artist to let her see the pieces and she would consider me for the exhibit. She's still a few weeks away from making the final decision on who gets the spot."

"What are you going to do?"

Kate threw up her hands. "I have no idea, Mags. I have no idea what it means to be more 'authentic' or paint with more 'authenticity.' Right now, I kinda hate that word."

"You'll figure it out," Maggie replied with full confidence as she flounced on the couch.

"Easy for you to say. You've made a name for yourself." Kate hated how surly her voice sounded. Her best friend was a talented sculptor with a loyal following who sold her pieces before they were even done. She'd worked hard to be where she was, but she made it look easy, and sometimes Kate felt jealous of her best friend.

Maggie looked at Kate and held her gaze.

"I'm sorry, I didn't mean to lash out. I just want this so badly." Kate dropped her shoulders.

"I know you do, Kate, and you'll figure this out. I have faith in you!" Maggie leapt up from the couch and gave Kate a side hug before skipping down to her room. "Do you need to use the bathroom?" she shouted down the hall. "I've got a date with Damon, and I need to get ready."

"THE Damon?" Kate asked. "When did he finally ask you out?"

"He didn't. I got tired of waiting so I asked him out for sushi. Sometimes you need to take the initiative in life rather than wait for the Universe to deliver."

Kate mulled over Maggie's words as she walked down the hall and stopped in her doorway. Arms crossed, she looked at her room through a different lens. Four empty white walls, beige carpet, a faded purple comforter wadded up on a single bed she'd had since she was twelve, a battered $25 dresser from the thrift store pushed against a wall, and an old yellow sheet covering her window in place of an actual curtain. Her easel occupied a corner next to a tv tray covered with tubes of paints and a pitiful collection of her most used brushes. It felt stark and bare compared to her aunt's. Maybe if she had a place like that to paint in, her pieces would be more inspired.

Kate's eyes widened and her pulse raced—whether in exhilaration or fear she couldn't say—as an idea took shape. She wasn't taking any classes this summer and she only worked part-time at the restaurant, which meant she had some free time. Her mom refused to step foot into her old childhood home, and there was no one else nor any other family, so she could, in theory, use her aunt's space to paint on her days off with no one the wiser. It would take her mom months to go through the courts to have Aunt Esmerelda declared dead and sell the house and land. It was the perfect plan. Nothing could go wrong. Nothing. Mind made up, Kate changed into her favorite jammies, crawled into bed, and fell into a restless sleep filled with nightmares that faded in the morning light.

2) Mrs. B

Kate's eyes darted over her aunt's expensive collection of brushes and ran a finger across the soft bristles. Her eyes closed in bliss at the luxurious feel. She felt a twinge of guilt using her aunt's supplies but brushed it off. Aunt Esmerelda would want her to use them rather than having them go to waste, or worse, get thrown out. Supplies of such caliber were meant to be treasured.. Now, where would the paint be? Kate turned and spotted an old, beat-up, three-drawer dresser against the wall and opened the top drawer. Wood dividers separated the drawer into sections, each one filled with tubes of paint in different colors of that hue like a rainbow. Reds and oranges in the top drawer, yellow and green in the middle, and blue and purple in the bottom drawer. Tubes of neutral colors completed the ensemble and filled two wire baskets on top of the dresser. Kate blew out her breath. The brand of paint her aunt used was expensive, the kind she only dreamed about using while buying the cheaper versions. Elation bubbled up at the thought of using these exquisite supplies, and she couldn't contain her smile.

She scooped up the jars that held dried paint and sashayed to the kitchen, skipping a few times on the way as excitement spilled over. Using her elbow to push the door inwards, Kate stepped into the kitchen and froze at the sight of a well-rounded woman bustling about in front of a stove. The aroma of fried potatoes and onions wafted from the cast iron skillet and Kate's stomach rumbled loudly. The woman turned and Kate froze for a fraction of a second before her shoulders dropped and her stance relaxed at the sight of the woman's gentle, knowing smile and eyes that showed recognition. Kate took in the woman's kind eyes, short, curly, golden hair and stopped at a familiar faded golden yellow apron as a name popped into Kate's head.

"Mrs. B?"

The woman nodded and a rush of warm feelings flooded Kate as she dropped the jars on the counter and ran over to hug her tight.

"Oh, Kate, my little one! How have you been? I can't believe how long it's been! Let me get a good look at you." Mrs. B held Kate at arm's length and looked her over from head to toe.

Kate gazed at Mrs. B as bits of memory played like a disjointed movie. She caught a glimpse of her younger self, wearing Mrs. B's coveted apron, stirring chocolate chips into a bowl. Flour covered the counters, floors, and the three of them—Kate, Mrs. B, and her aunt—while their laughter filled the kitchen. Another memory of Mrs. B as she sang and stirred a pot on the stove. Little Kate sat on the counter next to the stove, and she could smell the cinnamon and warm apple cider. And then she was kneading bread under the direction of Mrs. B who was saying, "Push and pull, dear. You're doing good."

"This is taking forever." Kate pouted her lips and dropped her arms.

"It does take some time and work, but I promise it's worth it. When it's fresh from the oven and warm, the butter and honey just melt into it. Mmmm. A bit of heaven."

Her aunt trudged into the kitchen from outside, covered in and trailing blue dust with every step. Little Kate jumped into her aunt's arms.

"I've missed you, Aunt Esme! Where did you go this time? Zuntaca? Omkreda?"

Aunt Esme's smile didn't quite reach her eyes, but little Kate didn't notice.

"No, dear one. This was a secret place."

"No fair!"

"I promise when you're older to tell you all about it. Now, what are you up to?"

The memories faded and Kate was pulled back to the present.

"Do you still like tea, dear, or do you prefer coffee now?" Mrs. B repeated.

Kate rocked back on her heels in disbelief. Who else had she forgotten from that summer? Her eyes grew wide as a thought struck her.

"Have you heard from Aunt Esmerelda? Do you know where she is? Do you know how to get hold of her?" Kate's questions spewed out at Mrs. B.

"My goodness, Kate. Slow down. I haven't seen Esmerelda in almost a year. She travels a great deal and sometimes she's away for months at a time with no way to get ahold of her. I don't ask where she goes, and she doesn't feel the need to tell me. Now, why the forlorn look? She always comes back."

"You don't understand, Mrs. B. My mom plans on having Aunt Esmerelda declared dead so she can sell the house."

"Your mother can try whatever she likes, but this house has been in your family for centuries and isn't going anywhere," Mrs. B said.

Kate turned and flopped into a kitchen chair. Obviously Mrs. B had never met the force known as her mom. "She already has a team of lawyers working on it. She's relentless when she wants something."

Mrs. B smiled. "I know what your mother is like, Kate. Tell me, though, when you heard what your mom planned, did you put up a fight?" Mrs. B's eyes held Kate's. Kate squirmed and looked away.

"She doesn't know I overheard her plans, and why would I put up a fight? My mom has more claim on the house than I do. She did grow up here."

Mrs. B sat down in the chair next to Kate. "You have a claim to this house as well."

"What do you mean?" Kate asked as her face scrunched in confusion.

"You don't remember?"

"I didn't remember you until I saw you and a few memories came back. I didn't even know how much I missed this house until I pulled up last night. Everything from that summer is blank. I don't remember anything."

"You'll remember, Kate. You're already starting to, and once a thing starts, it's hard to stop it, and then you'll do the right thing." Mrs. B got up and went over to the stove to stir the potatoes. "Now, if I remember, you like your potatoes a bit crispy. The bread is in the toaster and fresh honey is in the pot. Grab some plates and set the table."

Kate pushed her plate away and leaned back in her chair, stuffed. *Like a travit*, her mind whispered. An image of giant, six-legged, shaggy, bioluminescent creatures that rambled about and bellowed the most intriguing sounds filled Kate's head so clearly she almost swore it was a memory and not her imagination. She shook her head in wonder. She hadn't imagined things like that in a very long time. She squirmed in her chair, hearing her mother berate her, insisting she lived in the real world, not the imaginary ones she liked to make up. Being in this house dislodged more than memories it seemed. She turned her attention back to the present.

"Thank you, Mrs. B. That was delicious."

"You're welcome. You could show your appreciation by helping with the dishes before you go abscond yourself away in the solarium to paint."

"How did you know I came to paint?" Kate asked.

"The house told me."

"Houses can't really talk, Mrs. B. It's impossible."

"And what did your aunt say about impossibilities?" Mrs. B reached out and grabbed Kate's hand, eyes never leaving hers.

Kate shrugged.

"Humor me and try to remember, dear."

Kate sat back with her eyes closed and tried to remember what her aunt said. Minutes ticked by as she searched the recesses of her mind. She was just about to give up when her eyes flew open, and the words slipped out of Kate's mouth. "We're only limited by the realm of our imaginations."

Mrs. B smiled and patted Kate's hand. "There. I knew you'd remember. Now help me clear the table."

Twenty minutes later Kate stood in front of a blank canvas, eyebrows furrowed, arms crossed, the corner of her lip caught in her teeth, as she waited for inspiration to strike. Minutes stretched into an hour, yet inspiration eluded her. Kate eyed the tubes of paints she had chosen from the dresser. Maybe if she just started to play with them something would spark. She needed to see how these paints worked anyway compared to the cheaper paints she used in the past. Kate grabbed some blues and squeezed dabs onto her palette, mixing the colors with a small knife to create new colors. She swirled the sapphire blue around the wood board, lost in the ethereal feel of it as it moved across the wood. Her hand unconsciously picked a brush from her aunt's collection as if it knew what to do. The blues were jarring against the white but that faded as the white vanished under her brushstrokes. Hours later Kate stepped back, exhausted and exalted. This was the inspiration her work had been missing. The blues, so like the dust on her aunt's clothes, flowed across the canvas forefront, seeming to ebb and flow like the sea, but in solid form, or at least dust form. Three moons shimmered with iridescent colors, reminiscent of an oyster shell, and filled the sky above. One moon so close you could almost touch it, one further out, and another furthest away. The trifecta of beautiful moon goddesses. On the left side of the canvas, crystal formations towered and lifted their arms to the moons, reaching out for them, lovers forever torn apart. It felt like she could see the dust move and hear the crystals sing and her soul cried in relief at being set free from the shackles to create what it had always wanted to create.

She turned and noticed a tray containing a sandwich, wedges of apples, some cookies, and tea sitting quite patiently on the chaise across from her. *Mrs. B*, Kate thought with a smile. Her stomach growled and Kate was surprised by how ravenous she was. She glanced outside and saw the sun dipping behind the horizon. She'd been so consumed she missed lunch and dinner. She shoved half the sandwich in her mouth, followed by the glass of now watered-down, lukewarm tea. Even warm it still tasted wonderful as orange flavors tickled her taste buds. A yawn escaped as a wave of exhaustion washed over her. She pushed the tray aside and curled up on the chaise. She would just rest for just a minute before she left for the night.

A hand shook her shoulder gently and pulled her from a deep sleep. She mumbled something but then heard Mrs. B's voice.

"Dear, you fell asleep. Come now, I've put clean sheets on your old bed. You can sleep there for the night."

"I should really head home, Mrs. B." Kate pried open her eyes.

"Nonsense. It's late, and I won't have you driving home half asleep."

Mrs. B put her arm around Kate and guided her up the staircase tucked inconspicuously among the plants. They reached the top landing, walked down a short hall, and turned right, straight into a child's fairyland.

The room was large with a slanted ceiling, lilac walls, and colorful area rugs scattered over the hardwood floors. Art that ranged from whimsical to realistic covered every wall. A massive, old, handcrafted wood dollhouse took up space in one corner of the room. Kate's eyes were drawn to a movement in the other corner. Silk rainbow fairies twirled and danced as they cascaded down on strings attached to a mobile, but there was no wind or wind-up parts visible.

Mrs. B steered her towards a small bed under the slanted ceiling. Cream fabric with delicate pink flowers covered the wall and puddled on the floor behind the bed. Kate imagined herself surrounded by the fabric, closed off and protected from the outside world, as she read by flashlight. She crawled under the covers and sank into its embrace as Mrs. B stood at the end of the bed. "Good night, dear one. We've missed you."

Tears welled in Kate's eyes and threatened to spill over. She had missed them too, it seemed. Kate's thoughts drifted off as she succumbed to sleep's sweet embrace but not before she heard Mrs. B whisper into the room, "Help her remember who she is."

3) Miswala

Kate's eyes opened as she became aware of her surroundings, not sure what had disturbed her sleep. She sat up and looked around at fuzzy dark outlines, but nothing seemed amiss. Sleep pulled her back down, but just before she closed her eyes a flicker caught her attention. She propped herself up on an elbow and strained to see in the dark. There! A tiny flicker from the painting on the wall in front of her. A frown pulled her lips as the flicker bobbed and wove its way down the painted path, growing larger and larger until it resembled a prepubescent child and floated down from the painting. No, not floated. Flowed, like it was suspended in an invisible pool of water.

Mesmerized, Kate watched its long hair swirl and dance around its face, convinced it must be a dream. It inched closer, eyes locking with Kate's, and Kate decided she was done with this dream. She threw the comforter over her head and squeezed her eyes shut, feeling a sense of security in the childish gesture. Seconds that felt like hours passed in silence, broken only by the soft exhale as Kate slowly let out the breath she had been unconsciously holding. She thought about bolting for the door but knew she lacked the nerve to abandon her safe burrow. She stayed there, alert for any movement, until she heard a faint sound. She strained her ears and caught it again. Music. Soft, lyrical, intricate notes that wove together and told a story of familiarity. The music washed over her as it grew to a crescendo, releasing rigid muscles as her fear melted away. She sat up and threw the comforter off, coming face-to-face with the apparition.

Kate peered closely at its grey body—grey eyes, grey hair, grey skin—encompassing all the shades of grey Kate knew along with others she'd never seen. These greys weren't flat like living room paint though. These greys were beautiful and stunning and had depth. These colors flowed and chased each other to the cadence of the song and Kate sat transfixed until the haunting melody song ended and it smiled at her.

"I knew it was you," it said.

"You knew it was me?" Kate repeated, head tilted, mouth drawn down.

"I felt you. Your energy's changed, but I knew it was still you."

Kate searched the apparition's face for answers. "Are you a ghost?"

High-pitched, merry tinkling notes filled the air as the apparition giggled in amusement and shook its head.

"What are you, then?" If it wasn't a ghost, it must be a dream. The problem was it didn't feel like a dream. It felt real, which was impossible.

"You don't remember?" The creature's shoulders dropped as deep, solemn notes replaced the merry tinkling.

"There's a lot I don't remember apparently." Kate shook her head and wondered why for the first time.

"You used to call me a friend," it said with a wistful smile.

Kate pursed her lips and jutted her chin towards it. "I would've remembered you-" she started and stopped. Would she have? Hadn't she forgotten Mrs. B and earlier wondered who else she had forgotten? Yet this couldn't be real. So instead, maybe it was her subconscious trying to tell her something.

"Can you fill in the blanks?"

The apparition smiled faintly and shook its head. "So much is about self-discovery and that has to start from within."

"There's not much to discover about me besides a few lost memories." Kate snorted, annoyed as she rubbed her forehead. All this talk about remembering was giving her a headache.

The apparition sighed. "You're going to do this the hard way, aren't you? You always were stubborn, like Merelda." It gestured for Kate to put her hands up.

"If I refuse?"

"That's your choice, Kate. It's always been your choice."

Kate hesitated a full thirty seconds before she reluctantly raised her hands, palms facing outwards.

The apparition gently placed its palms against Kate's. Kate's eyes bulged as energy coursed from the creature's palms to hers. She felt the current fill every inch of her body. She looked down to see the hair on her arms standing up, and felt her hair floating around her face, yet she was not afraid. This was like hugging an old friend you hadn't seen in forever. One you had forgotten how much you adored. Kate closed her eyes to feel it more deeply and a vision took shape, of little Kate sitting on the same bed, in front of the same apparition, giggling as her long hair floated around her head like a cloud.

"You're amazing, Miswala! I wish I could do that," eight-year-old Kate exclaimed.

"All of my people can do it. It's quite easy for us," the apparition responded.

"When can I come visit you?" Little Kate asked as she shifted from side to side.

"When Merelda allows it."

"She won't, you know. I've asked and she ALWAYS changes the subject." Little Kate's bottom lip quivered.

"Merelda will know when you're ready. Until then I'll come visit you here," Miswala promised.

"Can you teach me a song, Miswala?" Little Kate cocked her head and changed the subject. She knew Miswala would never go against her aunt.

"I can try. Human voices don't quite have the range we do."

"You mean like this?" Kate let loose a screech that made them both dissolve into giggles.

The memory faded, and Kate looked at Miswala.

"How's this possible? What are you?" Kate's eyes widened, and her breath came in faster and faster. "Maybe it's stress. Stress has been shown to play tricks with the mind. That has to be it. Stress has been shown to play tricks with the mind."

"Sleep, Kate. Everything will reveal itself in time." Miswala flowed off the bed and towards the path in the painting with a backward glance.

"I'm not tired." Kate yawned as her eyes closed against her will and her breath slowed and returned to normal. She laid down and barely managed to tug the covers back up.

"Poor Kate. Yours is not an easy road, but you must remember. Merelda needs you." Kate heard before she was lost in the sweet oblivion of sleep.

The next morning Kate woke to the warmth of a small, long-haired, black cat curled against her belly. The cat stretched on its side and pawed at her hand, and Kate smiled. She scratched behind its ears, and purrs rolled off its chest like a loud freight engine. She reveled in the feeling of contentment emanating from its small body, and for a brief moment, everything was right in her world. Last night's encounter faded in the light of day. It had to be a dream, maybe an old childhood dream, brought on by staying in her old room. Remnants of an active imagination she'd had as a child.

Unbidden thoughts of who would take the cat broke her reverie, and she sighed. She'd be sure to ask Mrs. B about the cat and any other pets her aunt had. She rolled out of bed and with a final swipe down the cat's back and over its floofy tail, headed to the kitchen where she hoped she would find Mrs. B.

She stopped just before the kitchen door, as she heard two distinct voices coming through the door. She recognized Mrs. B's voice, but the male voice wasn't familiar. She loitered by the door and listened. She reasoned she wasn't eavesdropping but just being safe by not entering a room where she didn't know one of the people.

"It's been a long time," a man's voice said.

"I'm quite aware of how long it's been, but she's here now," Mrs. B's voice replied.

"But . . ."

"No more of that. Things have already started."

Kate's curiosity got the better of her and she pushed through the door. "What things?"

"Getting this family back together," Mrs. B replied blithely. Before Kate could question her more, Mrs. B turned towards an older gentleman. He wore denim overalls, had thinning white hair and was holding a pair of gardening gloves.

"Do you remember Mr. H? He's taken care of the grounds and the house for almost as long as I've been here."

Kate shook her head. "I'm sorry, I don't remember you."

The man shook his head, a pained smile pinched his lips.

"It's okay, Miss Kate."

"Are those blueberry muffins?" Kate asked, eyeing the overflowing plate, eager to move past the awkward exchange. She wanted to tell Mrs. B about the dream but asked about the cat instead.

"Does my aunt have any other pets?"

"She doesn't have any." Mrs. B brought the plate of muffins over with a deft hand and put them on the kitchen table. "Would you like some juice?"

"But she has a cat," Kate insisted, picking at a muffin as she shook her head. "I woke up with a black cat sleeping next to me."

Mrs. B smiled. "That would be Miss Luna, and she is most definitely not a pet."

"What is she then?" Kate asked.

"A friend. Now, will you be staying again today?" Mrs. B expertly changed the subject. "I think being here is good for you. I can make up the room again. You used to love it as a child."

"I don't think so," Kate replied as she set the muffin down. An undercurrent of energy, just below the surface, still pulled her to the house. The urge to stay was overwhelming but she needed time away to examine everything that had happened.

"I work the next couple of days so I can't, and I have errands to run so I should really head back home now. Thanks for the muffin."

Mrs. B replied, "Anytime, dear. We'll be here when you come back."

"You and who else I didn't remember?" Kate mumbled under her breath as she headed for the solarium to grab her things. She wasn't sure what she had expected when she first pulled up to the old house, but the past couple of days were not it.

A few moments later she slid into the driver's seat and tossed her purse on the passenger seat where her phone slid free, black and silent. In all the excitement she forgot to charge her phone. Which wouldn't have been a big deal except for her mother who needed to hear from her every day. Kate groaned. This was the longest she had gone without texting her mom and she dreaded the notification that lurked in her phone. Maybe she could say she lost her phone? Or never turn it on again? Did she even need a phone? Kate sighed. Maybe she could tell her mom she got caught up in painting? That excuse would irk her mom since she hated the career path Kate chose, but what else could she say? The truth? And risk being banned from the house?

That would send her mom over the edge and Kate didn't have the energy for that fight.

Kate started the car, plugged in her phone, and braced herself. After a few minutes the notifications came flying in. Thirty missed calls and one hundred and sixty-five texts?! Her mom had outdone herself this time. She put the car in gear but hadn't made it a mile down the road when her mom called. She pushed the Bluetooth speaker button and her mom's frantic voice filled the car.

"Kate? Oh, thank god! Where are you? Are you hurt? DO I NEED TO SEND THE POLICE?"

"Mom, I'm fine. I don't need the police. Really, I don't."

"Then why haven't you texted me or called me back? I've been worried sick thinking you were dead in a ditch or worse!"

"I'm really sorry but my phone died and I didn't notice."

"You didn't notice? For two days? What have you been doing? Who have you been with? Are you seeing someone?"

"Mom, no. I'm not seeing anyone. I was busy painting ok? I'm trying to get into a show and I really need to wow the owner. I've been focusing on that." Kate slowed the car as it rounded the corner and took a few breaths. "Look mom, my life is getting busier and there are times I may not be able to get back to you right away, which is normal. I have a job and I'm working on my career—"

Her mom snorted, but Kate continued. "I'm sorry I made you worry, and I promise I'll do my best to get back to you when I can, but there may be times when I'm too busy. You know I don't always have my phone on me." The palms of Kate's hands were slick with sweat and she rubbed first one, then the other, on her jeans. Why was it so hard to stand up to her mom?

"This doesn't sound like you Kate. Is there something you're not telling me?"

Thoughts raced through Kate's head and she panicked. If her

mom sensed she was hiding something she would be merciless in extracting the information. Sometimes Kate thought her mom worked for the CIA in a past life. "Of course not." Kate's voice cracked and she rushed on. "It wasn't intentional mom. I lost track of time and my phone but I'll try to be better. Promise."

"I see." Kate winced at the silent accusations behind those words. Her mom continued, "Now that I know you're not dead I have to get ready. Your dad and I are going out. We'll talk about this later." She abruptly ended the conversation. With a sinking feeling, Kate knew there would be hell to pay at a later date. Unlike Kate, her mom never forgot anything.

4) Dasme and Flora

Kate chewed her bottom lip as Morgan inspected her new painting. She tilted it under the sleek track lights that hung from the ceiling and murmured under her breath.

"You steered away from the abstract I see."

"I just painted what came to me." Kate clasped her hands together to keep them still.

"It looks like you found your muse. This piece is exquisite. How many more do you have?"

"Just the one. I wanted to make sure this is what you wanted."

Morgan turned to face Kate. "It's not about what I want. What I want doesn't sell. I mean, it does, but not if you're creating pieces based on what I want rather than creating pieces that make your soul sing. It's about finding what inspires you, what lights your passion, what makes you feel whole and connected."

Kate contemplated Morgan's words. Painting at her aunt's house did make her soul sing in a way that hadn't happened in years.

"I found a new spot to paint that makes me feel . . . I don't know. I love to paint, and it's always been a passion, but when I paint there it's like . . ."

"Like you are doing exactly what your soul purpose is? That's what happens when we find what we are born to do, and it's a rare thing to find. The majority of people are swayed by societal or familial pressures about what your life should look like instead of what it should look like for you." Morgan examined her painting again.

"I'm starting to figure that out."

"It shows."

"Does this mean you like the painting?" Kate tried to keep her voice even.

"It means I want you for the featured local artist spot at the show," Morgan replied. "You've proven you have the talent and can tap into that inspiration. Don't lose it. I'm going to need ten pieces—"

"Ten pieces," Kate sputtered. "There's not enough wall space for ten pieces."

"Please don't interrupt me; it's rather rude. I need ten so that I can select the top three I think will do the best at the event. I'll give you two weeks to decide. You need to think about if this is what you want, and if you can deliver before I waste my time on PR."

"I can answer now." Of course she would do it. It was her dream and nothing could stop her from doing this show,

"Don't. I've been burned before by artists who decided it was too hard and gave up. I like you, Kate, but I want you to think about this. Do you have what it takes to bring your art up to this level consistently? Call me in two weeks and let me know what you decide."

"I will. Thank you," Kate replied and walked out, feet barely touching the cement. She had barely finished texting her best friend *"have news usual spot in 10?"* before Maggie replied with *"already here."*

Kate slipped into the seat across from Maggie and tried to hide her smile, but Maggie was too astute. She took one look at Kate's glowing face and shrieked; heads turned their way. She grabbed Kate out of her seat in a tight hug that only best friends will understand before she let go and sat down.

"I got you your coffee, girl, so spill it."

Liquid lava filled her mouth as she gulped the coffee down, chased by the ice water Maggie handed over to her.

"You never could wait for it to cool. So, tell me! I'm dying to know!"

"She wants me to be the featured local artist at the event." Kate grinned and felt the warmth flood her body.

Maggie screamed again and threw herself onto her friend across the table, as coffee cups threatened to topple over.

"Oh my god, that's fantastic news! I knew you had it in you! Are you going to quit the restaurant once you become famous and sell out worldwide?" Maggie asked with a huge grin on her face.

"I'm not quitting quite yet. We have to see how the show goes," Kate said. Her cheeks hurt from the grin that hadn't left her face since she got the news. It was still hard to believe.

"What's wrong?" Maggie asked worriedly, as Kate's face fell.

"I painted that piece at my aunt's and used all her supplies." Kate's shoulders slumped at the realization.

"What's the problem?" Maggie asked, brow furrowed.

"I don't have those supplies anymore. I mean, I guess I could take the brushes and paint, but it was the space that inspired the piece. How am I going to find another spot like that in two weeks?" Kate's stomach clenched. Nothing would be like the house.

"Can't you just go back to the house and paint there? Court cases can take months and by the time your mom's done with it, you'll already have your pieces for the show." Maggie sipped her coffee and raised her eyebrow at Kate in a challenge.

"I don't know how long these things take. It could take months but with my mom? Knowing her, she'd find a way to speed up the process and get it done in weeks, not months, and it's not like I can ask her about it either. If I do, she'll know something's up and ferret out everything." Kate looked down and tried to tamp down the excitement at the thought of going back to the house. She'd only been gone a few hours and already missed it.

"Everything? We are just talking about the painting, right? Or is something else going on that you're not telling me?" Maggie's eyes narrowed and she cocked her head at Kate.

"I haven't told you about Mrs. B and Mr. H have I?" Kate questioned. She launched into the details surrounding their meetings, leaving out certain details. She knew Maggie would have questions Kate didn't have answers to.

"Well, you'll have to go back at least once to get your aunt's art supplies before the house is sold. You can't leave them to be thrown out. Use that day to paint something else and see if it's really the space that inspires you. And, of course, I'm coming with you. I need to see what all the fuss is about. A house your mom grew up in but hates, an eccentric missing aunt, and you? Don't tell me you haven't noticed how happy you are after you come back from that house. You glow, girl! Now, you know I'm not taking no for an answer. When do we go?"

Two days later Kate stood beside Maggie in her aunt's driveway and grinned at her friend's open-mouthed disbelief. If Maggie had any say Kate would have called off work and they would have left straight from the coffee shop. Instead, Kate had used the time to convince herself she had let her imagination get the best of her. Never mind how irritable and moody she had been since being away from the house. That probably had more to do with the wonderful memories she had uncovered about her aunt and Mrs. B and her desire to uncover more. Nothing more or less.

"This is amazing, Kate. Everything's amazing. I don't even know where to look first. It feels so different too, like fairies are going to pop up and whisk me off." Maggie gazed around and tried to take it all in.

Kate's smile faltered at the thought, but she quickly recovered. No one was going to get whisked off and everything was going to be normal this time with Maggie here.

"Just wait until you see inside." Kate grabbed Maggie's hand and pulled her into the house. "Upstairs first. Conservatory's last, since it's the best room in the house."

Heavy footsteps and laughter echoed down to the kitchen.

Mr. H glanced at the ceiling with somber eyes and then back to Mrs. B.

"I told you she'd be back. She can't ignore the house; it's in her blood. Janice can't erase that, as much as she would have loved to," Mrs B said as she threw flour down on the counter.

"But everything's gone all wrong. Esmerelda's been gone too long this time, and her sister wanting to sell the house. What happens if she does it?"

"You know as well as I do the house won't let that happen," Mrs. B replied curtly.

"But—"

"No more buts," Mrs. B said and dropped dough on top of the floured counter. "Now, I believe you have some plants to prune."

Maggie's eyes took in the expanse of glass and the endless view of the gardens. "It reminds me of an old English movie. One where the heroine gets killed, or was it the one where the house was haunted and everyone disappeared?"

Kate laughed, "So you don't like it?"

"I'm in love with it! I can't believe your mom grew up here and wants to sell it." Maggie twirled around to take it all in.

"I know. I don't get it. This house is amazing! I just feel so good in this room, like I can create a masterpiece given enough time," Kate said.

"And you shall!" Maggie replied with confidence. "Show me where the magic happens."

Kate walked Maggie over to the art nook and beamed as Maggie oohed over the space and view.

"Any idea what you're going to paint?"

Kate pulled a fresh canvas from the pile against the wall and placed it onto the easel. "No idea," she replied, already lost in ideas.

Maggie turned towards the back garden. "I think I'm going to explore a bit outside if that's OK. Some of those flowers I've never seen!"

"Don't get lost out there. The gardens look like they go on for miles." Kate smiled at her friend. It was no secret Maggie loved flowers. Kate knew they inspired her to create, and Maggie would prefer to be alone with them and her imagination.

"I have an internal compass, remember?" Maggie replied with a grin.

Kate picked up a brush and was vaguely aware of Maggie as she headed out the back door. Hours later she put her brush down and gazed at a portrait of Miswala, resplendent in all the colors of grey Kate could mix. Elated, she stepped back to view it from different angles, when it dawned on her that Maggie never returned. She swooshed her brushes in the jar of clean water and wiped them off on a cloth before she stored them and slipped out onto the back patio. A moss-covered path beckoned, and she followed it, passing by her aunt's expansive herb garden filled with plants she recognized—the hibiscus, which shouldn't be blooming this early, and the lavender—

but also exotic ones that didn't come from the local hardware store. Gigantic, twisted flowers that swirled like ice cream cones and changed colors from bright to burnt orange as the sun touched its petals towered over her. Small delicate bells, no higher than her ankles, beckoned to her with their lovely dainty smell of fresh dreams.

Kate jerked. What did fresh dreams even smell like? That sounded ridiculous to her but none the same, that was exactly how the flowers smelled. Kate pushed on and followed the path through the cottage garden thick with flowers, haphazardly grown. Some vibrant, others pastel, yet the colors and chaos seemed to work in a cohesive feel.

The path dipped down around a cluster of tall trees, like a gaggle of very old friends. She got the feeling she had interrupted their conversation, which was silly, but the silence as she walked past was unnatural. The path led her down a sloped hill and through an opening in a tall hedge fence that stretched in both directions, until the path finally ended in front of a concrete water fountain. An orange sphere bobbed and turned on top, its brilliance undiminished by the water that spilled over its edges and down two tiers, before it pooled into the bottom basin. Kate fought the urge to dip her toes in the water and instead turned her attention to the five paths that led away from the fountain. One felt familiar so she chose it and followed as it wove its way through a plot of massive magenta flowers on long spikes that resembled fluffy marshmallows. Kate reached out and marveled at the softness, drinking in their intoxicating fragrance and became transfixed as a memory came loose.

On this day they had been playing hide-and-seek for hours and were heading back to the house. Her aunt lifted her up to smell the flowers. "Don't they smell heavenly, Kate? These traveled in the pocket of your great-great—I can't even begin to count—great-grandma to here."

"Where did they travel from?"

"I'm not sure, bean."

"How come you don't know?"

"That information was lost years ago and there's no one around to ask."

"Well, if it's lost you can find it. You're the best at finding things. You always find me when we play hide-and-seek."

"That's because you giggle like a gaggle of kerflufkins."

"You're silly, Aunt Esme. But you could find it, if you just tried."

"I wish it was that easy. I've tried, but sometimes things are just lost and there's no way to find them." Her aunt set little Kate down on the ground. Little Kate slipped her hand into her aunt's and looked up at her with wide eyes. "What if you couldn't find me?"

"I would search for you forever and a day and look for you until my last breath," Aunt Esmerelda said and little Kate knew she would.

"I would search for you too! Even if it took me till I was old, like twenty-five."

Aunt Esmerelda's peal of laughter filled the air as the vision cleared.

Kate's throat constricted and she choked back tears. Life wasn't that simple. She wasn't eight anymore and the harsh realities of the real world had set in. There was no way she could look for her aunt now.

Guilt washed over her as she thought back to when she first found out her aunt was missing. Her dad had told her about it but couldn't give much information at the time. Afterwards, she had been so wrapped up in her own life—moving out, school, trying to get out from under her mom's thumb—that she barely asked her mom about it. Of course, her mom seemed reluctant to talk about it, which made it easier to ignore. Instead she assumed the police would take care of it. Even if she wanted to start looking now, too much time had passed. Where would she even start? She was only one person and she had a job, and a show to prepare for. Honestly, what could she do? She wasn't some detective protege, who could waltz in and find her with three clues found on her old clothes. No, she needed to focus on the present and find Maggie.

Lost in her inner turmoil, Kate turned a corner and almost smacked into a slumbering giant's head that blocked the path before her. Her feet stumbled back as she strained her neck up and took in the face towering over her. Soft, tall grasses covered its head and swayed in the breeze, giving it movement. Short, compact, fragrant, white flowers created eyebrows and dark green moss covered its face—its closed eyes, plump cheeks, and a partially submerged nose. Her fingers brushed the soft moss and Kate wondered who had labored over this landscape masterpiece and why it was tucked away at the end of the path instead of being on display. It reminded her of the heads at the Lost Gardens of Heligan, only much larger. Not that Kate had ever been to see them in person. Her mother hated traveling anywhere. No, she had only seen images on a computer screen when she was younger, which was completely different than standing in front of one. If she closed her eyes, she could almost feel the earth rumble with its slumbering breath and expected its eyes to pop open, as it lumbered out of the ground that held it in its embrace.

"Halt! Who goes there?" a tiny voice broke Kate's reverie. Searching for the voice she circled the head.

"Where are you?" Kate called out.

"Down here! Open your eyes, ya daft girl, and state your name and your business."

"Oh!"

Kate looked down and beheld a tiny mouse, resplendent in a dark blue uniform. It held a tiny gold staff and stood guard inside an open doorway twice its size, carved into the back of the giant's head, partially obscured by the willowy grass fonds. Kate made out a colorful landscape behind the mouse and craned her neck to look more closely when the mouse pounded the ground with his staff.

"I said state your name and business!"

"How are you talking?" Kate peered down at the mouse and looked for a way to explain its movements. Maybe it was a puppet? Or a lost pet? A young child, perhaps, that had dressed it up and lost it? And what? Taught it to talk? Or maybe mental health issues did run in her family, like her mom always said, or maybe the stress of it was just too much for her. Maybe this was all a hallucination. She seemed to be having her fair share of them in this house.

"Answer me or face the wrath of my staff!"

Kate burst into laughter at such a tiny threat.

"You dare laugh at me while I hold the staff of Anacafrey!"

The indignant mouse aimed its staff at a low-lying tree branch. Kate swore the air rippled in front of the limb and seconds later the limb shattered. She ducked to protect herself from the flying wood shards.

"What did that poor tree ever do to you, Dasme?" another voice demanded. Kate gawked at the other mouse dressed in puffy silk teal trousers, a silk yellow button-down shirt, and tiny socks and shoes that covered its tiny feet.

The mouse called Dasme in the blue uniform stomped its tiny foot and turned its nose up in disdain. "I had to, Flora. She's an intruder and I had to protect our village."

"She would have gone her own way without even seeing you. Now you've gone and frightened the poor girl. Really, we were entrusted with the staff to protect our home, not this. How are you going to explain this to her next time she comes around?" Flora sighed at the destruction of the tree.

"I'll tell her the girl was going to destroy our village, which she might have. You never know when the door gets stuck open what can come through," Dasme said.

"The only thing small enough to fit through the door is a squirrel," Flora argued.

Kate closed her eyes, rubbed her temples, and rocked her upper body. "This isn't happening. This isn't real. There were not talking mice—"

"What's she doing, do you think? I knew she was daft. Or deaf maybe? IF YOU CAN HEAR US—" Dasme shouted.

"Stop it. She's not deaf or daft, are you, dear?" Flora patted Kate's shoe.

Kate reluctantly opened her eyes and peered down at the mice. They stared back with concern as Kate muttered to herself.

"It must be too much stress. Stress does crazy things to people. None of this is real. Animals do not talk, and they most certainly do not blow up trees. Either that or I'm having a breakdown," Kate said as she shook her head.

"What's a breakdown?" Flora asked Kate.

"It's when there is a period of overwhelming mental stress—" Kate stopped. "Why am I explaining myself to a hallucination? You can't exist. The only rational explanation is that this is a hallucination brought on by stress. I mean I guess I could have lost my mind, but I still feel sane. Although maybe people still feel sane when losing their minds. How would I know, though; I've never lost it before."

"Do you need help finding it?" Dasme cocked his head at Kate.

"Finding what?" Kate asked, distracted by her thoughts.

"Your mind. You said you lost it. Flora, I really think this girl is daft." Dasme turned towards Flora and with his paws up.

"She's not daft. What's your name?" Flora asked and put a paw on Dasme's mouth to stop the words that threatened to come out.

"Kate."

"OK, that's a good start. Kate, what are you doing out here?"

"I'm looking for a friend." Kate turned and looked around the path, but Maggie was still nowhere to be seen.

"Don't you have any? Why would you try to find one out here?" Dasme asked bemused as he pushed Flora's paw off his mouth.

"Let me handle this," Flora said with a stern look at Dasme and turned back to Kate. "Did you both come from the big house?"

Kate nodded her head.

"Then you must know Esmerelda," Flora gushed.

Kate nodded her head again slowly and asked Flora, "Do you know Esmerelda?"

"Of course! We've known Esmerelda for years. She's the one who gave us the staff to protect our door."

Kate sat down abruptly in front of the small open door.

"Have you seen her lately?" Kate asked, not quite believing she was questioning talking mice about her missing aunt.

"I'm afraid not. Last time we saw her must have been about a year ago." Flora's paw stroked her chin. "The same time she gave us the staff to guard our door that gets stuck open."

"How long has it been stuck?" Kate watched through the door as purple and green clouds floated by.

"Off and on for about a year. It used to happen only once in a while, but now it happens multiple times throughout the day," Dasme reluctantly said, still eyeing Kate.

"That's when Aunt Esmerelda went missing." Kate peered more closely at the opening. "Can't you just close it?"

"Don't you think we tried that?" Dasme snapped.

"Pay him no mind, Kate, he's always grumpy. You of all people should know how doors work."

"What do you mean?" Kate asked as her pulse quickened.

"MARCO! GIRL, WHERE ARE YOU?"

Kate stood up and spun towards Maggie's voice.

"POLO! I'M OVER HERE! YOU WON'T BELIEVE WHAT I FOUND."

Kate turned back towards the mice, but they were gone along with the door.

"There you are! I've been looking for you everywhere!"

Maggie stopped short at the look on Kate's face.

"What's wrong?"

"Do you see any mice?"

"Are you serious? You better not be playing with me." Maggie hopped from one foot to another as her eyes scoured the path for rodents.

"No, not regular mice. These were—" Kate paused. Special mice dressed in renaissance clothes that talked. She sighed. "Never mind. Let's get back to the house. I finished a painting and I think you'll like it."

"I know I will. I keep saying this place is good for you."

Kate grimaced. That remained to be seen.

Maggie studied the painting as Kate watched, a fingernail clamped between teeth.

"I love this one! It's fluid, like it'll just flow right off the canvas and puddle on the floor. How did you get so many shades of grey? It's spectacular, Kate. You can't deny your talent now, not with this piece. You are definitely going places, girl."

Kate soaked in Maggie's words and beamed.

"I'm glad you love it as much as I do."

Kate's stomach growled and she glanced at the clock on the table. "We forgot to eat dinner."

As if on cue Mrs. B appeared in the doorway. "Dinner's ready, girls."

Kate looked over at Maggie. "It would be terribly rude not to eat since she took the trouble to cook for us."

"Terribly rude," Maggie replied. She hooked her arm through Kate's and dragged her off into the direction of the kitchen. They each took a seat around the kitchen table, beautifully set with lit candles that glowed and created a warm ambiance.

"Mrs. B, I seem to remember you regaling Aunt Esmerelda and me with stories full of adventure, or am I remembering that wrong?"

"No, you remembered correctly."

"Would you please tell us a story?" Kate asked, wanting to take her mind off the events of the day.

The candles flickered and cast a shadow over Mrs. B's slight smile of assent. She began. "The bees knees held a different meaning for George and Harriet. In fact, it held different meanings for most ornabees . . ."

Kate and Maggie sat transfixed, lost in the words and worlds spun by Mrs. B. The kitchen table became a bubble of suspended time and reality, a haven from the stress and pressures of life, while the outside world trudged on.

5) Chirp and the Journal

As much as I'd love to stay, I should get home and get some sleep." Maggie rose from the table. "Thank you, Mrs. B. The story and food were amazing. Are you sure you don't need any help cleaning up?"

"My pleasure, Maggie, and you can help clean up next time. You know you're always welcome here and I always have lemon cookies stocked for people I like."

"Don't tempt me, Mrs. B. I already have a food baby that's feeling pretty heavy right now." Maggie rubbed her belly for emphasis and smiled.

"I'll grab my stuff," Kate replied as she stood up from the table.

"You stay here," Maggie instructed. "I already scheduled an Uber and they'll be here any minute. Stop." Maggie held up her hand at Kate's objections. "Go and paint while you can, girl. I'll be sleeping by the time you get home so I'll see you tomorrow."

They walked to the front door.

"Are you sure, Mags?" Kate asked.

"I am. I have to get to bed early tonight. Love you, girl." Maggie replied.

"Love you too," Kate said. "Make sure you text me a picture of the driver and when you get home, please, so I know you made it safe."

Maggie smiled and reached for a hug, but Kate jerked back and peered down the dark hallway.

"What is it?" Maggie turned her head and looked behind her.

"Nothing. I thought I saw something, but it's probably my imagination." Kate shook her head.

"Another mouse I suppose?" Maggie laughed.

A car honked from the driveway.

Maggie hugged Kate then opened the door and stepped through. She stopped on the top step and looked over her shoulder at Kate. "Go paint a masterpiece," Maggie said and bounced down the steps and into the waiting Uber.

Kate closed the door with her back and stood up straight. Her eyes scoured the walls and willed it to move again. Minutes crept by and self-doubt started to eat at her when the creature scurried halfway up the wall from the shadows and stopped. It was small and pink, just the length of her hand, with three sets of elongated eyes (all staring at Kate) and three sets of thick legs that stomped up and down—first one side, then the other—in excitement, reminding her of a puppy. Its small round mouth chirped before it scampered down the hall.

The creature stopped and waited while Kate's mind grappled with what to do. Should she follow the now blue-patterned chameleon who blended seamlessly with the wallpaper, or turn around and leave the house for good? After all, the hallucinations had started with the house. Maybe if she left they would go away too. Except Kate wasn't too sure about that. It felt like life could never go back to the way it was before, and would she even want it to?

Her mom's unwelcome voice invaded Kate's head.

Kate, it's the house. It's feeding into your imagination. You've had issues with this in the past. None of this is real. It's impossible.

Her mom's sharp voice faded as Aunt Esmerelda's voice tugged

Kate into the past. Soon a memory took shape.

The two lay on a blanket and gazed up at the night sky. Inky darkness settled over them like a blanket, a darkness you can only find outside the cities, devoid of light from street lamps, parking lots, businesses, and homes. The kind of darkness where you feel yourself fall upwards and get lost amongst the stars. And on this particular night, stars filled every inch of the night sky, each one more brilliant than the next, as if putting on a show for the humans below who were deep in conversation.

"Did you know that we're made up of stardust?"

Little Kate rolled her eyes at her aunt. "How can dust come from the stars? You just told me the seven sisters were four hundred light years away, so how can their dust come all the way down here?"

Aunt Esme smiled. "It happens when a very big star runs out of fuel and dies. It explodes, sending elements into space, which are 'seeds' for new stars and planets, like Earth."

"So Earth is made up of bits from a big star dying?"

"In a way, yes, and humans are also made up of those elements as well."

"It just doesn't make sense to me, Aunt Esme. It seems impossible that we're made up of the same stuff no matter what you tell me."

"My precious Kate. There are things in the worlds that your mind will balk at. Things it will say are impossible, but never forget, impossible is just a limit of your imagination. If you were to go back in time a hundred years and tell people there was a machine the size of your palm that could answer any question in the world, show you what a planet out in space looked like, or go on a virtual museum tour in another country, they would think you mad. Things we couldn't even comprehend a hundred years ago are now commonplace, not even given a thought, due to science, our imaginations, and people willing to test the boundaries that constrained others. Can you imagine how different our world would look if inventors, explorers, artists, creators, or scientists would have let

impossibilities stop them? People on the edge of greatness aren't held back by impossibilities, Kate, and you shouldn't be either."

Kate took a deep breath. Everything may seem crazy and unbelievable right now, yes, but she had never felt more alive! Every single part of her body tingled and the hairs on her body stood up. She wanted to see where this led, which meant she needed to follow that little chirping creature to see where it took her. She spotted it on the floor, the movement from its rounded bottom giving it away, as it pounced on a rogue dust bunny. Laughter erupted from Kate at the absurd yet adorable sight. The creature tilted its head sideways and chirped before it scurried back down the hall. She strode after it, spotting it in patches of light before it disappeared in the darkness, only to reappear in another patch of light. Door after door passed until she almost missed it slithering under one and stopped short. She stood before an old door, carved with swirls and spheres, worn where hands rested as they pushed it open. How many of her ancestors had touched this same exact spot where her hand now rested? Slowly she pushed the door inward and, peering in, stepped through.

Kate took a few more steps into what appeared to be her aunt's study. Tall, built-in bookshelves covered three walls, overflowing with books of every shape and color, books that beckoned to Kate. She ran a finger over some of the spines and tried to decipher the titles, most of which were in another language. Strange symbols decorated other book spines. Artifacts from her aunt's travels were placed amidst the books, each one telling a story that only her aunt knew.

Unwilling to dwell on that thought, Kate turned towards the center of the room where a large, solid, regal, mahogany desk stood at attention. Facing the desk were two soft, brown, leather wingback chairs, worn at the armrests and bottom, that would befit even the weariest of travelers to sit a spell and tell their tale. Another leather chair sat behind the desk, with less wear than the others, as if the owner spent more time on their feet than sitting. A large stone fireplace, big enough to walk into, covered the wall behind the desk and Kate imagined sitting there with her aunt, deep in conversations about life, while the fire kept them toasty. A rug, worn thin in spots, covered the hardwood floors. Muted shades of red, orange, and brown added even more warmth to the room.

Kate sat down in her aunt's chair and examined the desk. The rich wood top, like so many things in the room, showed wear from generations of use. Three drawers lined both sides equally, six in all, with a smaller drawer in the center to hold pens and such. Papers covered one corner of the desk in a haphazard pile, as if her aunt had just popped down to the kitchen for a quick bite and would be back any minute. An old antique radio occupied another corner of the desk, with a spiral shaped speaker that adorned one half with the other half full of knobs and dials. In the middle of the desk furthest away from her aunt's chair sat a peculiar music box made out of pulleys and gears that sat next to a pair of binoculars and an old brass compass. Kate traced the letters N, S, E, W and wished they could point her in the direction of her aunt. She rifled through the papers hoping for some clues, but they seemed to be written in the same strange symbols and writings that many of the books held. Kate groaned in exasperation. The cute little chirpy creature scampered up her leg, tilted its head and chirped at her in concern.

"I'm OK, Chirp. I would just like some answers," she replied, as she easily slipped into conversation with it.

Chirp let out another chirp in answer before it turned and leapt off her knee onto the desk. Kate watched as it scampered to the back panel before disappearing. Intrigued, Kate pushed the chair out of the way, and crawled on all fours to get a closer look. Sliding her hands over the wood, she searched every inch and there, ever so slightly that she almost missed it, were tiny slivers of depressions. She rocked back on her heels and whacked her head on the underside which did nothing to dampen her excitement. Kate heard of desks with secret compartments but had never actually seen one in real life. Her fingers deftly searched the underside of the desk for a way to open the compartment, but she came up empty.

Vibrating with excitement she clambered out of the small space and proceeded to pull the drawers out and empty their contents onto the worn rug. She ran her fingers over every inch of the drawers, followed by a search of the empty drawer slots. She frowned at the desk, willing it to give her answers but it remained silent.

She looked up at the music box now at eye level. An intricate metal spider sat atop a tall box covered in gears and pulleys of different shapes and sizes. The spider sat, its eight tiny, delicate, mechanical legs frozen in front of its abdomen, waiting for something. Kate's eyes followed the pulleys, searching for a beginning, when she spotted a tiny keyhole, made for a tiny key, in a tiny corner.

Kate remembered seeing a small box filled with tiny identical keys and tore through the jumbled drawers until her fingers clasped the box. Time slowed as Kate tried each key, her pile of discarded keys growing, until finally, the second to the last key fit.

She carefully turned the key a few times and let go as the pulleys and gears turned. Fascinated, she watched the spider pull a delicate thread from the bottom of its abdomen and weave a tiny, intricate web. It stopped and there was a soft pop as the secret door opened slightly. Kate held her breath, heart hammering in her chest as she stuck her hand inside and felt something hard. She pulled out a travel-worn leather-bound book, straps tied in a knot, and sat back in the seat to work at them. As the last knot fell away, the book opened to the first page, and she recognized her aunt's handwriting from birthday and Christmas cards. Unconsciously she tucked her feet underneath her body in the chair and began to read as the words ran off the pages, swirling around Kate, and images played like a movie as her aunt's voice began to speak.

6) Esmerelda's Travels

I don't know who will find this (one can hope and prepare but that is all) so I will start from the very beginning. Of course, the beginning of my story, not the very beginning of how the worlds happened to be. That would be presumptuous at best, ignorant at worst since no one knows how these things started, or how they work. Physicists and scientists would tell you what I know and have lived through is impossible, but that's only a limit of their imagination. Science is real, but it changes as we understand and learn more of what is out there in *our* universe, never mind the others.

But, I'm jumping ahead of myself and the story, as does happen quite often with me. Which makes writing down this story following a linear path difficult for me. My mind wants to jump around and focus on other things, and it is dreadful to try and sit for a time and not do anything else but this. But it needs to be put into writing. Historically, that is how stories are passed on, ones that we don't want to die at least, and I do not want this to die with me. That would be a travesty. So let's jump in, dear reader, and start with when I was just a little girl, living in this house, with my little sister and both my parents.

Ours was truly a magical life. We spent our days exploring the world around us as we played pirates in the creek, explorers finding new lands, or we would wear our very best and fanciest fairy wings to have tea parties in the garden. My father loved to join in and would pretend to be a wild beast and chase us, as our little girl screams dissolved into belly laughs. We were whole, and loved, and safe, as every child should be.

When the weather didn't cooperate, we created plays and acted them out for our parents or whiled the day away immersed in art—painting, drawing, sketching, pottery. My little sister had so much talent. She never did believe me when I told her she was better than me. Such a shame, really, she could have . . . well, never mind. Her story is not mine to tell. Mine is the only one I can pass on. To whom? That remains to be seen, as I have no children of my own to leave this to. And fear not, I am not sad about my non-child status. I don't think I would have made a very good mother at all. What I am sad about is this will all end for my family line. I had hoped . . . well, it doesn't matter what I had hoped, does it? I cannot see the future, but I can trust in what I know and believe.

So onward with my story.

I didn't mean to become a traveler, although it did change my life and made it ever so much more interesting. I shudder to think that could have been my life. How ever do people live like that? Work Monday through Friday, eight to four if they're lucky? Nothing to look forward to, except weekends of kids, carpools, and home renovation shows? That is certainly not my cup of tea and sounds absolutely horrid. I know some thrive in that environment, but I would have withered away. Of course, who's to say that would have been my life? Perhaps I would have been an activist seeking change. Or an entertainer, thrilling millions with my death-defying acts. Or traveled the world, living moment to moment, not caring a fig what the future held. But again, I digress. My life didn't end up like that, and it certainly has been anything other than boring.

From a young age, I knew my family was different. My mom would be gone for weeks at a time and the only thing anyone said was she was away on a trip. Never where or for how long, or what she did on them. I always knew when she was leaving though. The air felt different, heavier. One day she would be there and the next she would be gone. Much later I found out my dad tried to shield us from certain aspects of our lineage. He wanted us to have a normal life, which my mom tried to respect. While I understand his desire, I think so much would have been different if they would have been honest from the beginning and let us each make our own choices. As it was they decided to leave it up to fate. If we stumbled through a door we became a traveler like mom, and if we didn't, we would live a more normal life, like dad, who never wanted to travel. As if our lives could ever be normal. I think if my father had lived longer, things could have been different, but sadly he didn't. When he died from a heart attack, we had no other family. No grandparents, aunts, uncles, not even a distant cousin. All we had was what used to be a small, close-knit family, with no one to lean on. Our family crumbled as the weight of our grief affected us differently.

Jani, who was only six, took it out on me. She felt cheated and angry that I got more years with our father. She stopped playing with me and spent all her time alone. Whenever I did attempt to talk to her, she shrieked so hard and loud, her eyes and throat bulging, forcing me to cover my ears and flee.

After a week she lost her voice, so she switched to pretending I wasn't there. I could handle the shrieking, but the silence sliced through my heart each time she ignored my pleas. My mother, for her part, preferred to stay in bed for weeks on end and wrap herself in her grief like a cocoon. I begged her to get up, shouted that we needed her, but nothing pierced her grief. I was alone and things were spiraling out of control.

Left on my own, my desire to escape consumed me as I wandered our property, venturing further and further every day. Maybe I had a distant relative who would swoop in and rescue me. Or my teacher would take me in from class like in that movie *Matilda*. I just wanted to escape all the hurting so badly. The pain, the sadness, the loneliness, all of it, I just wanted it gone.

On one of these walks, I let my mind empty and watched my feet as they crushed the grass beneath them, step after step, mesmerized by the cadence. It felt like I walked for miles when the grass shimmered like a heat wave mirage and turned into fluffy clouds on the ground. I wasn't sure if I imagined it or if it was real, but it felt so good to have fun again, I didn't care if it was real or not. I jumped from bouncy cloud to cloud, like a trampoline, and jumped so high up in the air I thought I was flying. On one of my trips up, I spotted giant dragonflies as they darted over a field of flowers so massive they took my young breath away. This new world made me feel so alive and electric and amazed that I forgot all about my pain for the few short hours I spent there.

Eventually I knew it was time to go home and I slipped back through the shimmering door, trying to burn its location into my brain. For the first time in my young life, I contemplated running away. I desperately wanted to go back to my new world and live there. I could do it, since there was no one left to care anymore, but who would take care of Mom or Jani? What would happen to them? I walked home with heavy steps, deeply absorbed in thoughts too big for a nine-year-old until my feet paused on our side porch as my brain took a second to register music.

Upbeat music poured out the door and I strained my neck around trying to make sure I was at the right house. What if that door brought me back to a life where my family wasn't broken? I forced my heavy feet forward and opened the door, wincing as the screen door slammed behind me. My mom—who hadn't cooked for weeks—was at the stove and whirled around at the snap from the wood. I took a step back, startled by the broad smile and giddiness as she rushed over, grabbed me in her embrace, and spun me around, laughing the entire time.

"You clever, clever girl!" she gushed, out of breath. "You found a door!"

"How do you know I found a door?"

"The air feels different when someone goes through one. An almost imperceptible shift. It's a skill you'll pick up quite easily. Oh, Esme, I have so much to show you, so much to teach you about all the different worlds!" She set me down and twirled me around.

"There's more than one?" I gasped, dizzy with the possibilities and the twirling.

"So many you can't even begin to imagine." She stopped twirling me and grabbed my hands.

"Have you been to a lot of them?" I asked.

"I've been through thousands of doors." She held my gaze and smiled.

I cocked my head as a thought took root. "Is that where you go when you leave? Through the doors?"

"Yes, baby. I travel and explore all the other dimensions. Like our ancestors before us. And now you will too! It's in our blood, Esme, your blood." She stood back up and stirred the pot on the stove.

"What's in our blood?" I asked, looking down at the blue veins in my arms.

"Traveling. Traveling is in your blood. You come from a long line of travelers through my side of the family."

"Really?" I asked, wide-eyed.

"My mother—your grandmother—was a traveler, and every generation before her had a traveler for as far back as we know." She came back over to me, eyes dancing with excitement. "I know this is a lot to take in and you must have questions but let me tell you what I know first. It's going to be hard to believe but we're not from here. We're from another planet in another dimension—"

"Another planet? Wait? We aren't human? Is that why we never go to the doctors? Why did we leave and come here?" I asked, confused with this new information.

"Esme, let me finish! Our ancestors had to flee our home before it was destroyed. They barely got out alive."

"How was it destroyed? Did they come here through a door? What was our planet called? Can we go back? Do we have any other family? Can Jani do this too?" I sat down on the floor of the kitchen as my imagination took off with the possibilities.

"I don't know, I assume so, I have no idea, I don't think we'd want to, no and maybe. Now, enough questions! Tomorrow we begin your training, but tonight we celebrate!" my mom exclaimed as she danced around the kitchen again.

"What's going on?" my sister asked as she walked in and eyed us up and down.

"We're celebrating!" My mom exclaimed.

"What are we celebrating?" Jani asked as her face lit up, hopeful.

"We're celebrating Esme. Your sister and I will be leaving soon to go on some trips," my mom said, too wrapped up in the prospect of traveling with me to treat Jani gently.

"Can I come?" she asked as her lips trembled.

"You're too young, Jani. Maybe in a few years. Until then I've brought someone to stay with us to watch over you while we're gone. Would you like to meet her?"

Janice shook her head, eyes darting between me and our mother as she backed up.

"Things are going to be different," our mother crowed as Jani slipped out the back without a sound.

And things were different. Mrs. B came to live with us, and mother and I started my training. She taught me things that had been passed down from prior generations as well as what she had learned on her own. How to look for doors, what worlds were safe, which ones were inhospitable, how to communicate with others, how to blend in to keep yourself safe, how to fight, what weapons were best in each scenario, and on and on it went. We were rarely home during the following years. I think it was easier for my mother to stay away than deal with her grief, and honestly, I was glad for the escape as well. Unfortunately, that left Jani alone with Mrs. B and she became even more sullen and withdrawn and like a stranger. I begged my mother to show her a door so she could join us, but she was adamant that Jani had to discover one for herself. She insisted it had always been done that way and if shown a door before a person was ready, it would be detrimental. She never elaborated more on that.

When I was twenty, mom died tragically—caught in a door as it closed— and left the house to me. Jani begged me to sell it and move with her. She argued it would be a fresh start for us, but I couldn't. She thought I chose the house over her which wasn't true. This amazing house is special, which is why it's always been in our family and must remain. The house and property sit upon an intersect of energy lines and vortexes, making it an extremely powerful place. A place where those same energy lines and vortexes create doors that we use to travel to other dimensions. Of course, there are doors all over the world, but here, here the energy is concentrated and powerful. I suppose that's why my ancestors chose to build here. Unfortunately, that same powerful energy ebbs and flows and is not always consistent. Doors can stay open for years or for a fleeting moment, and there's no way to tell. I've spent decades finding them and traveling through them, and even I don't even know where all of them are. Only the house knows that, and it won't tell. After centuries it's absorbed some of the energy it sits on and has become somewhat aware. To what extent I'm not sure as it likes to surprise me.

As for my life, I truly love it and wish everyone could experience this level of happiness.

Especially Jani. I so wish things could have been different. I wish she would have found a door or that my mother had allowed me to show her one, but she gave up believing in anything but the mundane a long time ago and I can't say I blame her. But she does blame me and sometimes I think she hates me. I've tried over the years to mend our relationship, but she just shuts me out. When she got pregnant I had hoped, well, it doesn't matter what I'd hoped.

But I digress again. After my mother passed away, I continued to travel and explore new worlds, made new friends, and enemies, saved lives, and learned so much about all the dimensions and universes around us. Information I'm about to pass on to you, dear reader.

And now you know the backstory, dear heart. I hope you continue to read on as it is bound to get more interesting as I tell my tales of my travels. After all, someone needs to know. Without further ado . . .

Kate closed the book with a soft thud and sat in silence. Her aunt's words swirled together in a chaotic mess that Kate didn't have the energy to untangle. The way Kate saw it, there were two possibilities. One, her aunt was as delusional as her parents had hinted at her entire life. In that scenario Kate was in very real danger of losing her grip on reality as well. The second, as impossible as it sounded, was that this was all real. Lately she'd been learning that impossible had no meaning here, but traveling to other dimensions? She couldn't even wrap her brain around that one and didn't want to try. The only thing she wanted was to sleep and not think, but what to do with the journal? It didn't feel right taking it out of the house, and since she worked she wouldn't have the time to read it. She fought the urge to call off and forget the rest of the world so she could stay and read more, but that wasn't an option. The restaurant was short-staffed, and Kate needed the money. The only choice left was to put it back where she found it, where it would be safe. She'd be back after her shifts to read more.

After putting the journal back, she made her way to the kitchen where Mrs. B always seemed to be.

"I'm done for the night, Mrs. B. I'll be back Monday morning."

"I could make up the bed again."

"No, really, I need to get home. I work double shifts this weekend so I'll just see you Monday morning."

"I'll have some of your favorite blueberry pancakes waiting for you," Mrs B said with a smile.

"Thanks." Kate lingered at the door, torn.

"Was there something else?" Mrs. B nudged.

Kate hesitated a split second before she replied, "No. See you Monday."

She wasn't ready to ask Mrs. B about her mom and Aunt Esmerelda's past. She couldn't process anything more tonight. The ride home was uneventful, and Kate fell into her bed fully clothed, and stayed awake just long enough to kick her shoes off before the sweet oblivion of sleep swept over her.

7) Kate Dreams

Kate ran through a field of the thick, waist-high grass that grabbed her legs and slowed her down. She was terrified, trying to run from something but didn't know what was chasing her. She tried to stop but her legs kept running, running, running. She looked over her shoulder and saw blackness, utter and complete, devouring everything in its path as it came for her. Kate wasn't sure how, but she knew if it consumed her she would forget everything about the house. All the memories, her aunt, Mrs. B, all of it. She screamed *No* but barely a whisper came out. Tears streamed down her face and her chest heaved with the exertion.

Up ahead she spotted the house and sobbed in relief. If she could just reach it, she knew she'd be safe. A moment later, warmth enveloped her as she went limp and was lifted into the air and carried towards the house. She rather absently noticed that she was tethered to the house by a faint stream of energy, and that's what was pulling her in. Her hands tried to grasp the cord, but her fingers slipped through the energy over and over again. Huh. She knew she should feel afraid but instead felt a sense of belonging and love. In a blink she was deposited gently into her aunt's study. A figure with short auburn curly hair sat in the chair and studied a piece of paper that looked like blueprints. The figure looked up with familiar green eyes and Kate started in surprise.

Aunt Esmerelda smiled. "My clever bean. I knew you'd find it."

Was she talking to Kate?

Aunt Esmerelda's smile turned somber. "He mustn't get his hands on it. It must be protected at all costs." Aunt Esmerelda glanced over her shoulder and back to Kate. "He's coming. Don't let him find you. Go!" Her aunt's face twisted into a scream as her face turned pale and gaunt and the walls closed in on Kate. She frantically searched for a way out as a giant clock loomed over her, laughing maniacally. Her legs sunk into the floorboard and she struggled to break free as everything came crashing in around her.

Kate bolted upright in bed, drenched in sweat, heart pounding against her chest. Moments passed as the dream lost its sharpness and her breathing returned to normal, until the only thing that remained was a sense of foreboding. It was just a dream, right? Kate squirmed under the weight, got out of bed, and headed for the shower. She hoped she would be too busy at work to think about dreams or journals or the questions they raised.

"Miss, I need sugar for my coffee. No, that's not what I want. I want the blue packets. That is too sugar. Oh, excuse me, a sugar *substitute*."

"Hey, I need more syrup. This one's out. You guys never give enough syrup." Even though it was full when she set it down at the table fifteen minutes earlier.

"Can I get more napkins, this isn't enough."

"Do you get free refills with milk? Why not? It should be."

"I'd like the #2 but with bacon instead of sausage and no pancakes. No, I don't want the #3. Oh, wait, that is the #3, sorry."

Towards midmorning her manager approached her.

"What's going on with you, Kate? You're distracted and you've been short with our customers, which isn't like you. There have been some complaints, which I can't have."

"I'm sorry, George. I have a lot of stuff on my mind right now."

"Well, stuff your stuff down. Everyone has stuff but people come here to get away from stuff and you're bringing your stuff to their tables, which they don't want or need. Got it? Good. Now table four needs more butter."

"I'll get it after I greet table seven," Kate said.

"Fine. Just hustle. Morning rush is done but you still have to fill the condiments before the lunch rush."

Kate walked over to greet table seven and stopped in confusion as a perfectly coiffed woman sat in the booth. She wore dark jeans and a button-down black silk blouse, and her brown hair was cut in a straight bob, not a hair out of place. A few pieces of tasteful, expensive jewelry and impeccable makeup completed the look which put her out of place in a family diner where the breakfast specials were $4.99.

"Mom? What are you doing here? Is Dad here?"

"No, it's just me. You've been avoiding me, and I wanted to talk to you. I thought this would be the best place to get your undivided attention."

"Mom, I haven't been—"

"Ahp, yes you have. You haven't been returning my phone calls or answering my texts even after you promised to do better."

Kate looked down at her order pad, unable to meet her mom's eyes. "I've been busy, Mom." She looked at her manager, eying her from behind the counter. "My manager is right there, so what can I get you?"

"Coffee first, if it's any good. Second, I know you overheard my conversation with the lawyers about the property."

"I don't have time for this right now," Kate said and scribbled coffee on the order pad and prayed for her manager to come and interrupt them.

"Then when would be a good time to talk? All those times I called and texted and you never responded? No? Fine. Then we'll talk here. Look, there are things about that house, things you don't know about, things that are none of your business. Both my mother and sister were mentally unwell, and that house is partially to blame. I won't go into details but suffice it to say it's a good thing it's going to be razed for condos.

Kate clenched her teeth against the vomit that rose in her throat as her mom's eyes flicked to her jaw. "Don't clench your teeth. You look feral."

"You can't do that. That house has been in your family, OUR family, for generations!" Kate exclaimed.

"Why do you care?" Her mom's shrewd eyes searched Kate's.

Kate dropped her gaze to her server pad and focused on keeping her voice even.

"I just think, what if your sister comes back and the house is gone? I mean she could still come back. We don't know what happened to her. What did the police say when you reported her missing?"

Her mom's eyes slid down to her watch as she checked the time. "My sister is not coming back, and I do not want to have this conversation again," her mom replied, evading the question.

"If you hate the house and your sister so much, why did you leave me there for an entire summer?" Kate's voice rose and customers turned towards the table.

"Hi ladies, how are we doing today?" Kate's manager sidled up to the table with a fake smile affixed to his face.

"We're fine, I just realized I'm not hungry, so I'll just be leaving." Her mom shot a look at her that spoke volumes.

"I'm so sorry to hear that. Was it anything we did?" her manager fawned.

"No, I just suddenly lost my appetite. If you'll excuse me." Kate's mom scooted out of the booth and walked out without a backward glance to her daughter. Kate grimaced as her stomach churned and thought the weekend couldn't get worse, but she was wrong.

Sunday night as she left the restaurant, she spotted her dad by her car. She approached him with a cautious smile and waved.

"What are you doing here?" Kate asked.

"We need to talk. Can we go for a walk?" Her dad's face spoke volumes and trepidation filled her body.

"Is Mom OK?" Kate asked as they walked across the street to the park.

"Physically, yes, mentally, not so much," her dad responded.

Kate cringed, knowing what was coming. "Dad, please don't. We had an argument, that's all."

"Yes, you did, and your mom's feelings were hurt pretty bad. She won't say it, but I will."

They walked down a paved trail under the sweeping oaks in silence for a few minutes.

"You asked your mom why, if she hated that house and her sister, she sent you there for the summer? Let's sit." Her dad nodded at a park bench. "My bones aren't what they used to be."

"You're a spry fifty-year-old."

Her dad's silence hung between, thick like a curtain until he finally broke it.

"I'm just trying to find the words here. They don't come easy. Now, your mom would flay me alive if she knew I was here talking to you about this. She thinks some things are better left in the past. But how can you understand the present if you don't know about the past? Your mom loved your aunt, but they always had a complicated relationship. Your grandma and aunt left your mom alone quite a bit, especially after your grandpa died. Getting rid of that house will be therapeutic for her." Her dad looked off into the distance. "Your mom never wanted you to find out what I'm about to tell you, and I've been too worried about how you would see me to argue. Do you remember that summer at all?"

"Not really."

"My job was stressful, and I often put in long hours. Your mom and I fought over that."

"I think I may remember that you weren't around a lot and it was just me and mom."

"What you don't know is that I spent that summer in rehab. The stress, the long hours, the fights with your mom, it was all too much, and I started drinking. It started small, I'd stop at the bar for a drink to fortify myself, and it grew. I hid bottles through the house and the last straw for your mom was when you cut yourself pretty bad on a broken bottle under the porch steps in the back. Your mom gave me the ultimatum: I either get my life together or she would leave me and I wouldn't be able to see you. She couldn't trust me to be a father." Her dad's voice broke. He took a few moments to gather himself and continued.

"I spent our savings on booze and the rest went towards rehab, which isn't cheap. Your mom had to get a second job to pay the bills and keep the house. I wanted to sell it, but your mom wouldn't hear of it. She wanted to give you what she never had: a stable home life. That woman worked sixty to eighty hours a week doing what she could to save our home until I got out of rehab and could work again. She sent you to stay with your aunt for the summer. She didn't want to but there was nowhere else for you to go. Towards the end she suspected your aunt's mental issues were rubbing off on you."

"Why did she leave me with someone she thought had mental issues?" Kate asked, not knowing what to think.

"She thought her issues were harmless. Her sister had a very active imagination and didn't have both feet in this world, if you know what I mean."

Kate jerked but her father didn't notice and continued.

"Your mom thought she was just a bit off is all. Until she noticed you were having trouble distinguishing between what was real and what was just imagination. She panicked, brought you back, and hired a babysitter for that last week. Once I came home, I got a different job, a less stressful one that allowed me to be home with you more, and your mom went back to school to follow her dream of becoming a lawyer." Her dad paused and then went on. "Your mom has worked tirelessly for this family. And after she brought you back, you got better too. After time you were able to see what was real and what wasn't, so it all worked out fine in the end."

They sat in silence a few more minutes as Kate mulled over her dad's words.

"I know your mom can be a bit much sometimes, but she does things because she loves you. Just keep that in mind." Her dad's eyes searched Kate's.

Kate nodded and stood up. Her dad's arms closed around her in a tight hug and Kate almost broke down and told him everything. He let go and the moment passed.

"Thanks for telling me. It couldn't have been easy."

"As long as it helps you understand your mom more, it was worth it."

A new fear niggled at Kate's thoughts as they made their way back to their cars. What if this wasn't real? What if she were like her aunt and couldn't tell real from make believe? What if . . .? Kate kissed her dad goodbye and drove home determined not to give the house another thought for the next few days. She toyed with the idea of seeing a therapist or telling Maggie but the idea of putting into words what had transpired made her uneasy. She didn't want her best friend thinking she was crazy. She would just lay low for a few days, see how she felt, and go from there.

8) Trilesk

Monday morning rolled around, and Kate struggled to move as exhaustion lay over her like a heavy blanket. Nightmares had plagued her all night. Bleary-eyed she glanced at the time. 5:00 a.m. She could either try to get more sleep (which she knew would be impossible) or try to get some work done since she still needed pieces for the show. Kate made a mental note to call and confirm with Morgan later. With everything going on it had slipped her mind. For now, coffee called to her, and she slipped out of bed, ran fingers through her disheveled curls, and padded to the kitchen to make a large pot.

While she waited for it to brew, she busied herself getting a cup and milk out. If she stopped too long sharp pangs would pull on her, pull her back to the house. Being away was painful and she wanted nothing more than to sit in her aunt's study and dive back into her aunt's stories while eating Mrs. B's lemon cookies, but she knew she couldn't give in. The house was like an addiction and Kate needed space to sort things out.

Coffee done, Kate poured a cup and went back to her room. She contemplated the empty canvas as inspiration eluded her. She blew on the coffee and took a sip before trading her mug for a brush. Soon paint oozed out as she smashed her brush into the canvas over and over, trying to force something, anything, onto the canvas.

A few hours later she flung her brush down in anger knowing the piece was a lost cause and couldn't be salvaged. It was no use. The pull of the house was just too strong to ignore.

Relief flooded Kate's body as she pulled in the driveway. *Home.* She didn't know how or why but she belonged here, and she couldn't deny that anymore. Kate let herself into the house and crept down the hall to the study, eager to delve back into her aunt's world. She took the key out of her pocket, pushed it into the spider, and turned it. Mesmerized, she watched as it spun its tiny web until it was done and the door popped open. Kate dropped down, scooted under the desk, and eased out the journal. She settled into her aunt's chair once again and opened the book. Words ran off the page and swirled around the room as her aunt's voice filled her head. A vision filled her mind's eye of a teenage Esmerelda in her old bedroom, hopping around, and the world tipped as Kate fell into the journal, further and further until she opened her eyes and saw through her aunt's eyes. She felt the wall with a hand that wasn't hers and tried to make a fist but couldn't. It appeared she was there just as an observer. Her aunt's voice filled the room, narrating the events as they unfolded.

I was sixteen when I fell through the door to Trilesk. I considered myself an expert traveler at the time, so it was very vexing to my young self to fall through, and not very elegantly either I dare say. One moment I was hopping around my room, pulling my boots on, eager to explore a new door I had discovered. The next I stumbled against my wall and fell through, flat on my stomach. I lay there dazed for a few minutes and tried to catch my breath in the middle of a blue dust cloud my appearance had stirred up. After I caught my breath—along with a mouthful of dust—I struggled to my knees. I called myself all kinds of names for not knowing there was an actual door in my room, but the names fell away as the sheer beauty of the planet struck me.

Lovely, dark blue, shimmering sand covered the landscape, broken only by large crystal formations. Tall, smooth, and ethereal, they reminded me of elegant, entwined dancers, arms stretching up to the sky in adulation. I lifted my gaze and my eyes grew wide and my hands scrambled for support as I fell back. Directly above me a massive moon filled the purple sky, incredibly close and heavy, and defied everything we knew about gravity, or what we thought we knew. I sat transfixed and watched iridescent colors as they raced over the surface and created a dance that rippled and swirled and left me breathless. A second and third moon were stacked further away, gorgeous colors I had never seen before. The closest I can describe it is varying shades of the most gorgeous pink you have ever seen, which doesn't do it justice but will have to suffice. Some things just don't translate well to Earth experiences.

I don't know how long I sat there mesmerized when a voice spoke and asked me what I was. I turned my head and saw a curious creature studying me. I looked down and saw myself as it saw me. Dark auburn wavy hair pulled into a semblance of a low ponytail, eyes hidden behind a special pair of dark welder's goggles made for our type of travel, a dark jacket with deep pockets, and boots. A far cry from the creature that stood, well floated since it had no feet, before me. It was grey, but not in the way you think. It wasn't boring, or flat. The creature was made up of *hundreds* of shades of grey and rippled through it from its hair that floated around its head, to its skin, to its wide eyes. Floated? That wasn't quite right. More like, it swayed and moved as if it was underwater.

"Can you not hear me?" it asked again, and I was quite surprised to hear music emanating from it, yet I could discern no instruments for it to play.

"Yes, I can hear you. I was just admiring your moon," I replied as I tried to discern where the music came from.

"It is rather beautiful, isn't it. How did you get here? We don't get visitors here, M'ra won't allow it," it replied, and studied me just as intently as light, curious, staccato notes filled the air between us.

"Who's M'ra?" I asked, intrigued.

"Only the Caretaker can tell you. Would you like to meet them? I'm sure they would want to meet you. You must be special since M'ra let you through."

"Yes please, I would like to meet your Caretaker."

Laughter erupted and high-pitched notes tinkled with mirth. "Not MY Caretaker, THE Caretaker."

Smiling at their obvious amusement I asked what their name was. "Miswala."

"Mine's Esmerelda."

It nodded, turned, and floated away, not waiting to see if I followed. Silence ensued for the rest of the trek, broken only by the happy music notes that trailed after Miswala. As we made our way over the sand, I thought of this Caretaker we were meeting. After seven years of traveling, I had developed a pretty good gut feeling and currently no warning bells were going off, but I remained vigilant.

We trudged on—walking on sand is difficult and hard and made the walk seem so much longer than it actually was—and came upon a small opening in the side of an enormous crystal formation. Miswala flowed right through the opening while I eyed the slit skeptically. I took a deep breath in, plunged through, and managed not to lose too much skin in the process, and fell into a small cave.

"Do you fall down a lot? Is that part of having those?" Miswala asked and eyed my legs.

"Not usually, but this is an unusual day."

Miswala turned, but not before I noticed a small smile, and

disappeared down a tunnel in the back that led deeper into the ground. I grimaced and trotted after the musical note that trailed up. After a few feet I noticed a glow from behind the thin crystal walls that lined the tunnel and became conscious of a hum, one so low I questioned whether it was real or not. I slowed my pace as the walls pulled my attention. A shiver ran down my spine and the hairs on my body stood up as I fought the overwhelming urge to touch the wall. My hands moved on their own accord, and I watched in slow motion as they splayed on the wall. I rocked back on my heels, my hands glued to the walls, and nothing in my travels prepared me for what happened next.

Energy burst through the walls into my palms and raced through every part of my body and mind as it sifted through every emotion I'd ever experienced, every memory, in a millisecond. It was if the energy was conscious, and wanted to know me through every moment that made me, me. It ended abruptly and left me soaked with sweat and shivering, yet also strangely exhilarated and energized. I felt more refreshed than if I had slept a solid eight hours, or been on the most relaxing vacation, or achieved the deepest meditative state. If I was honest with myself, which I always strive for, my body had never felt so alive. I vibrated ever so slightly from the residual energy and didn't want it to end. I looked around for answers and spotted Miswala who gestured for me at the end of the tunnel. With the newfound energy I caught up to Miswala easily, but before I could ask any questions they smiled and gestured into a cavern.

"Welcome to Trilesk, Merelda."

I stepped into an enormous chamber and gazed at a massive, upside-down teardrop-shaped crystal. It appeared to balance on its point with no visible support, which seemed impossible. Round tunnel entrances bored through the structure sporadically. Grey creatures similar to Miswala flowed through and around the crystal, like bees swarming a hive, only calmer, and the most breathtaking music filling the air. Intricate melodies flowed in and out, discordant harmonies that somehow came together, mixed together in music that reached my soul and rooted me to the spot. Miswala gave me a moment before they floated towards the crystal when I stopped them.

"I can't float," I said and pointed to my legs, "and I can't reach the tunnel entrance."

"What good are they then?" they replied quizzically.

"Lots of things, really, but it looks like we've attracted some attention," I replied as a trio of grey creatures approached us from the crystal hive. I studied them but could discern no obvious difference except one carried themselves differently. They all had the same long hair, and soft facial features. The two stopped a few feet in front of us but one flowed forward until it was a foot away.

"Miswala?" the leader asked, not taking its eyes off me.

"Aslame, this is Merelda. I found it on the surface."

"What were you doing on the surface?"

"M'ra sent me." Miswala twisted slightly like a child caught.

"M'ra spoke to you directly?"

"Not exactly, it was more of a feeling that I was supposed to go up there and it must have been right because I found Merelda," Miswala's greys darkened slightly, and I swear they blushed.

"I'll let it go for now, Miswala, but you know how we feel about you going up to the surface. Now, I believe you have duties to attend to." Aslame dismissed Miswala.

"Yes, Aslame," Miswala replied, reluctantly and floated towards the hive with a backward glance.

Aslame tilted their head for a moment, and listened to something I could not hear. Satisfied, it turned to me once again.

"My name's Aslame. I am the Caretaker. This is Osswa, my offspring, and Esmalt, offspring of my offspring." Aslame gestured towards the two creatures behind it.

"My name's Esmerelda, and I am the traveler."

"What does that mean, traveler?"

"What does that mean, Caretaker?"

A trilling of merry notes filled the air. "I like you, Merelda. I think we are going to get along just fine."

9) Miswala 1

Over the next thirty years, I visited Aslame and Miswala as much as I could. I shared stories of the outside world and my adventures and, over that period, learned a few things about them. I learned they were energy beings and that music was central to their life. Fascinating really. Emotions translated to music. The younger entities felt stronger emotions which made their range of music broader, but as they "aged," the strength of the emotions faded. That's why Miswala trailed music wherever they went, like a stream of consciousness, yet music escaped Aslame seldom. They did not experience all emotions, as far as I could tell. Love, sorrow, excitement, and maybe mild annoyance, but never jealousy, anger, hatred, pain, or fear.

That changed the day Miswala hurtled through the door between our worlds and set things in motion that changed lives.

"Merelda, Merelda! Aslame wants to see you!" Chaotic, discordant notes reverberated through the air.

"Miswala, calm down, please! The music is deafening!"

"I'm sorry, Merelda, but I can't! Everything is wonderful but we have to go now!" Miswala shouted and tugged my arm, unable to contain their excitement.

Within minutes, I was half dragged, half flown, not only through the door, but down the sands, shoved through the opening, and through the crystal tunnels before being deposited into the Caretaker's inner chambers.

"Aslame, we're here! Merelda's here!"

Aslame appeared, eerily calm in stark contrast to Miswala. "Thank you. You may take your place with the others."

"What is going on? I've never seen you all in such a tither," I said as I stood up.

"It's a very special day, Merelda. A rare birth that M'ra requested you be here for."

"Who's giving birth?" I asked, hoping my voice wouldn't betray my excitement. I am a traveler, after all, which I just realized I never properly said what a traveler does. I guess that would be useful information to have. You see, travelers collect information. Or at least that's what my family does. We collect information on each place we visit. We collect information on vegetation, habitat, inhabitants, food, culture, deities . . . basically anything and everything. We also collect stories. Stories from the inhabitants, stories told down through generations, stories that are written, stories that are told, stories that were lived, stories about our adventures, epic stories, and small stories. We are the guardians of those stories, so you can imagine my excitement at the prospect of learning more about Trilesk!

"M'ra has indicated you are to know everything, so I will do my best to explain it to you, starting with M'ra, since everything begins with M'ra. Planets, stars, suns, all of us. Without M'ra there is no life, and we would not exist. M'ra sends a piece of themselves to other worlds to start suns and stars." Aslame held up a hand to my questions. "Please don't ask how that is done, for we don't know. Only M'ra does, but because of this, M'ra's energy needs to be replenished. That is the job of the Kokshai; they replenish M'ra's energy. There is only one Kokshai and only one Caretaker of the Kokshai. The task of the Caretaker is to gather sand from the surface, imbue it with energy, and feed it to the Kokshai, who then transforms the sand into energy orbs which are used to replenish M'ra."

"Does this mean you're made up of M'ra too?" I asked as a thought occurred to me.

"Yes. We are made when a Trilesk goes before M'ra. If M'ra agrees, we meld a piece of M'ra with a piece of ourselves, which creates new life," Aslame said.

"And when you die? What happens then? Do you even die?" I asked, intrigued by the whole process of energy beings.

"When it's our time, we are taken to the surface. There we are transformed into Orarela which then falls up to our moon, Lisket—"

"Isn't that just floating?" I interrupted.

"Yes, but faster and with purpose. Once every few thousand years Lisket rains down Takkernu, which replenishes the crystals on the surface. The surface winds blow sand over the crystals, wearing the crystals down, and replenishes the blue sand that is needed to feed Kokshai that creates the energy orbs to replenish M'ra. Everything here on Trilesk is part of a natural cycle, and today is no exception."

Aslame paused and listened as the music rose in the other room. "It's almost time, Merelda. Today you are to witness the birth of a new Kokshai. A rare event which happens only once every five thousand years. We are all privileged to be able to see something so momentous. And, of course, you will be there tomorrow for the Choosing of new Caretaker for the new Kokshai."

"Why, won't you be the Caretaker for the new Kokshai?" I asked.

"A new Caretaker is picked every time there is a new birth. My family have been Caretakers for the old Kokshai for five thousand years. It's time for a new family line to be chosen."

"Won't you be sad?"

"No. It's a joyous celebration when a Kokshai is born, and I will always be a Caretaker of M'ra. Now we must go."

Aslame led me down a tunnel that opened up into the innermost chamber where I stopped, stunned. An immense, glowing ball of energy hung suspended in the air. Arcs of blue light flashed across its surface, and I watched mesmerized as the energy seemed to move and flow and ripple, almost as if it were alive. I forced my eyes to take in the rest of the tall chamber and noticed what appeared to be every Trilesk entity as they filled the area above and around, and eddied around M'ra. Thousands of voices rose in different melodies and pitches. They bounced off the smooth crystal walls, came together, then separated, and made my soul sing at the complexity of it. A flicker drew my attention to a large crystal dais directly beneath M'ra where a curious white creature sat. It was so still I almost mistook it for a statue, except for the slightest movement of its deep, squared-off jaw. A rounded belly stuck straight out in front of its two-foot-tall body with small round eyes and no discernible neck, ears, or arms.

"You must watch. I must go join my offspring and the offspring of my offspring to sing encouragement to Kokshai. I will come for you after it is done."

Aslame flowed towards the dais and Osswa and Esmalt. They circled Kokshai and their voices lifted and joined the others. Moments passed and the pitch changed and grew louder, more chaotic, and more fervent. The Kokshai unhinged its mouth wide open and bellowed notes I could barely hear but felt the vibration through my feet up through my body. I clamped my teeth together and kept my eyes glued to the Kokshai as its voice melded with the others and created music that is indescribable. Tears streamed down my face in both gratitude and sorrow, and I knew I would never hear it again in my lifetime.

As the music reached a roaring crescendo, a spark spread from M'ra to Kokshai, consuming its entire body, burning brighter and brighter until I was forced to close my eyes just as it all stopped abruptly and left an empty vacuum of silence in its space. This is what they meant by silence being deafening. The singing picked back up, softer this time, and I cracked an eye open to see a smaller Kokshai next to the older one. Aslame glided over as the others left, one by one, until a few hundred were left to sing.

"It's done. Can you stand?"

"I may need a minute for my legs to stop shaking. That was unlike anything I have ever experienced. What happens to the old Kokshai now?" I gestured towards the dais.

"The old one will soon be absorbed by M'ra."

A headache crawled its way over my temples.

"You should go home and rest. I'll send Miswala to gather you for the Choosing. Until then, Merelda."

The next morning, I rose before dawn, too excited to sleep, as you can imagine. I paced the length of my room while I waited for Miswala. Of course, I could very well have gone through the door myself but that would have been extremely rude since Aslame specifically stated Miswala would come for me when it was time. Those that are impatient for something wonderful to happen know what I mean when I say time literally slowed to a crawl. I mean not *literally* literally. That only happens with—well, never mind, that's another story. For this morning, each second hung in eternity before passing, and it felt like years before Miswala finally came through for me.

"Are you ready Mer—"

I was through the door before Miswala could finish asking.

"What happens in this ceremony?" I asked, eager for more information as we walked across the sands.

"Those of us like me who have not yet reached a hundred years will gather around the new Kokshai. When it's time, the Kokshai calls to the one, they will hear and become the new Caretaker."

I struggled to talk as we walked up a sand dune. "Does it take long for the Kokshai to choose a new Caretaker?" I gasped out.

"No. At birth it's connected to us all and sees into each one to be able to choose the perfect Caretaker for them."

A few seconds passed as the ground evened out and I caught my breath. "You must be excited that you might be chosen."

"I doubt very much I will be chosen. I'm not like the others," Miswala said. "I know I'm supposed to be. I know I should be, but I'm not. That day I found you, I'd been out exploring the surface, even though it's frowned upon. I was supposed to be singing to M'ra since it's what sustains M'ra."

"I thought the Kokshai fed M'ra?"

"The Kokshai replenishes the energy, but our singing sustains M'ra. It's hard to explain it to those who are not born Trilesk."

"So, you snuck out to spend time on the surface. I seem to remember you telling someone that M'ra sent you."

"Well, I'm not sure it was M'ra, but if I hadn't come up, we never would have met and that makes me sad." Small notes like falling rain fell from Miswala.

"It makes me sad too, as I value our friendship." Miswala's notes picked up and became joyful again.

As we entered the chamber Miswala lifted me into the tunnels, and we made our way into the inner sanctum where Aslame met us. I could see the younger Trilesks gathered around the same dais used in yesterday's birth, where the new Kokshai now sat. Miswala glided over to join the others with a backwards smile to me. The room vibrated with excitement at such a monumental event.

"Are you ready, Merelda?"

I nodded as the hairs on my body rose, whether in response to the energy or singing or something else, I couldn't tell.

Aslame flowed over to the pedestal and looked up as some unspoken communication passed from M'ra to Aslame. Aslame's voice emitted a single note, followed by others adding their voices to create a note that resonated and filled the chamber. The singular note sung by thousands was a far cry from the complex music of the birth, but it still stirred something within me. The younger Trilesks looked on with rapt attention at the Kokshai, whose eyes began to glow. The note dropped in pitch and the room reverberated as the note bounced off the crystals. I gasped and dropped to my knees as the vibrations pummeled my body. I clutched my stomach and fell to my side, and I caught sight of Osswa, offspring of Aslame. Even in my pain-fuddled brain I could see something was off about them, but I had no time to think about it. I struggled back to my knees just in time to see Miswala as they glided towards the dais before things swam out of focus and I collapsed. My body screamed as the vibrations reached a crescendo and for a second, I believed I might actually die, then it stopped suddenly. I lay on the ground, teeth clenched to keep the vomit down, while my body shook. A moment later the shivers tapered off and I won control of my stomach. I looked over and saw Miswala in rapt attention, hands on either side of the Kokshai, lost in their communication.

Aslame flowed over to where I lay on the ground. "Are you OK, Merelda?"

"Never better, Aslame. I may just need a few minutes on the ground if you don't mind. That certainly was not what I expected."

"I'll have Osswa take you home when you are ready. Be sure to get some rest. You may feel this for a few days."

I groaned, overjoyed at the prospect.

"Wasn't Esmalt one of the potential caretakers?" I asked, still on the ground.

"Yes, my offspring's offspring was a potential Caretaker, but it would have been highly unusual for the Kokshai to pick a line that were already Caretakers."

I stood up and swayed as fatigue hit me.

"I'm ready to go. Thank you, Aslame, for sharing so much the past two days. I'm honored and will keep your secrets safe."

"I know you will, Merelda. I trust you."

Osswa and I moved in silence that I broke once we got close to the surface door.

"I don't think I've ever gone this long in your company without you saying a single word, Osswa."

"I thought you would not want to talk. You looked unwell."

"I am exhausted, but I'm always up for talking. I'm sorry Esmalt didn't get chosen."

"It is the will of Kokshai," Osswa replied, as an undercurrent of faint, short harsh notes were snatched by the wind that started to blow. It was so out of character I thought I must have misheard it.

"Are you . . . angry?" I asked, bewildered.

Osswa stopped and smiled. "Of course not. This is the will of the Kokshai and M'ra. We are here." Osswa gestured towards the slight disruption in the air you could only see from certain angles. I opened my mouth to say goodbye, but Osswa was already gone. I stepped through the door when it hit me. I knew what looked off. At the Choosing Osswa looked bitter as Miswala approached the Kokshai and that was a look I had never seen on anyone from Trilesk.

10) Miswala 2

MERELDA, WE NEED YOU! The cry jolted me out of a dead sleep and echoed through the room. Wide-awake, I searched the darkened room, but nothing was out of place.

MERELDA, PLEASE! WE NEED YOU! Aslame cried. Before the cry stopped echoing, I had thrown on some clothes, instinctively grabbed my bag, and was through the door with a running start. A Trilesk appeared and pulled me through the sands without a word. The agitation that emulated from them bordered on panic and my heart dropped as I thought of Miswala and the others.

"What happened?" I spat out in between gasps of air.

The Trilesk didn't answer but picked me up and sped me through the rest of the way before they dropped me unceremoniously on the floor in front of Aslame, who was clearly agitated.

"Oh, thank M'ra you're here, Merelda! Miswala and Kokshai are missing!" Aslame moaned.

"What? Are you sure?" I asked.

"Yes, I'm sure!" Aslame trailed loud discordant music behind them.

"When did you notice they were gone?"

"I heard Miswala cry out from her room. By the time I got there it was empty, and they were gone. We've searched everywhere, even the surface, but there's no sign of them."

"Show me their room," I commanded, dread gripping my heart. You didn't cry out unless something was wrong.

Aslame led me next door, and I stepped through into a room carved completely out of crystal. A small dais for Kokshai occupied one wall; the other wall held an assortment of crystals, and a niche was carved out of the last wall, presumably for Miswala to rest. There were no doors or windows, save for the one we just entered through. Everything was as it should be. Except . . . that. A faint flicker by the back wall. I approached it and ran my fingers over the wall.

"What do you see?" Aslame asked quietly.

"A door was opened here."

"That's impossible," Aslame stated, even as uncertainty tinged their eyes.

I rummaged through my bag until I found the device I was looking for. A small holographic scene appeared as I trained the device on the wall. It showed the last few seconds of a dimensional door as it slammed shut. The signal was too weak to get anything more but at least it verified what I already knew.

"I'll need to talk to everyone who's had contact with Miswala since the Choosing." I stowed the device back in my bag.

"You don't think one of us had anything to do with this, do you? It's not in our nature, you know that." Aslame's shock was clear on their face.

"I don't see how it could have been done without someone's help."

"Everyone is gathered, Aslame," Osswa interrupted from the door; their eyes flicked to the wall where Miswala had been taken through and back down to the floor.

"I'll be there in a moment," Aslame said and missed the look of relief on Osswa's face.

"Is something wrong, Osswa?" I asked, a dark suspicion taking hold.

Osswa forced their gaze to the floor. "No, nothing. It is a difficult time."

I eyed Osswa and kept my voice even. "You keep looking at a very specific spot on that wall. A spot where someone opened a door, came through, and took Miswala and Kokshai. Why is that? Do you know something?"

"I di-di-didn't," Osswa stammered.

"Osswa?" Aslame's voice turned incredulous.

Osswa's eyes looked everywhere but at us.

"Osswa, I've known you for a long time," my voice softened and cajoled, "and I know you would never do anything to jeopardize your people. At least not on purpose. But now is the time to talk and tell us what you know."

"I . . . I . . . I can't."

"Kokshai will die without the sands to sustain them, and M'ra will die without the Kokshai. We will cease to exist! Suns and stars will die without replenishment from M'ra. Planets will wither and perish." Aslame drew themself up.

"Then it shouldn't have picked them!" Osswa let loose with a torrent. "Esmalt is more deserving! Miswala's not like us. They're different. You know that, Aslame. They were not worthy of being the new Caretaker!"

"What have you done?" Aslame whispered, as the grey drained from their face.

"He was only supposed to take Miswala, I swear!"

The air crackled as white, hot notes slashed through the air. Aslame's greys darkened as they cried, "Do you know what you have done?!"

Osswa cowered in the corner under Aslame's torrent.

"Aslame, stop! We need Osswa to find them to bring them back."

Aslame fought to control their anger and after a few minutes returned to their usual color.

I gestured to Osswa. "Start talking."

"When I was younger, I used to be like Miswala. I explored the surface and wandered for hours and dreamt of different worlds. One day I found a door and went through. I met someone who showed me their world filled with art and music and people, unlike anything I had ever seen. He told me there was more to life than wasting it all on M'ra and there were people who could harness M'ra's power for good, leaving us free to live our own lives. But I knew deep down that it was wrong, and I couldn't betray M'ra. I left and never returned. The door disappeared and I spent my life trying to make up for what I'd done. When the new Kokshai was born I thought it must be a sign I had been forgiven, but instead of choosing Esmalt, Kokshai chose Miswala."

Osswa paused before speaking again.

"The night of the Choosing I was so angry. I wandered the surface for hours until I stumbled on another door that led me back. I knew I shouldn't go through, but I felt so betrayed by M'ra. I wasn't sure what I was looking for or what I would find, but instead he found me. He was much older, but I recognized his energy, and he recognized me. We spoke for hours, or I spoke, and he listened. He told me he knew someone who could take Miswala away forever, leaving the way for Kokshai to pick a new Caretaker, a worthy one. He gave me a device that would open a door in Miswala's room and said they would take care of the rest. So I did and came up with an excuse to visit Miswala's room, placed the device, and fled. They were only supposed to take Miswala. Kokshai wasn't part of the deal. Oh, what have I done?" Osswa wailed as mournful notes filled the chamber and threatened to rupture my eardrums.

"Osswa, stop!" Aslame's voice boomed.

Osswa's mournful notes turned to whimpers as they cowered in the corner.

Aslame looked at me as I turned the information over in my mind. "Merelda, can you find them?"

"I think so, but first we need to send someone to watch the door. I'm not sure why they wanted Miswala or what they plan to do but if they think they can grab more of you, I'm certain they will try."

Both Osswa's and Aslame's faces drained at the implications.

"What do we do if someone comes through?" Aslame asked.

"Hide. The opening blends in with the crystals so they shouldn't find it," I said.

"If they do?"

"Let's hope they don't." I grimaced at the thought. "I need more supplies. Osswa, come with me. I need detailed descriptions of the city and the man you met. Aslame, I'll meet you back at the door in twenty minutes."

And with that I strode towards home, and then a new world.

11) Thargon

Kate became aware of her surroundings bit by bit as she came back to herself. She blew a breath out in disbelief as her body shook. She had felt everything as if it had happened to her instead of her aunt. The rough sands, the singing, the energy, the gripping fear when Miswala went missing, all of it.

She glanced down at the open journal in her lap and gasped. There in watercolors was a familiar scene, one she had painted not that long ago: blue sands, tall crystals, and three moons. What did this mean? Did her aunt tell her about Trilesk? Take her there? Is that why it felt so real? Was it possible? Kate wasn't sure of anything anymore. The line between impossible and possible seemed to get blurred in this house.

She desperately wanted to call Maggie, but what would she tell her? How could she expect her best friend to believe her when she barely believed it herself? Instead, she headed outside to the gardens that seemed different today and let her feet carry her aimlessly until she happened upon a long, wide arbor covered in dainty, fragrant, black and silver flowers. Her feet carried her in, and she heard rustling from above—or was that whispering—that stopped every time she did. Within minutes the end of the arbor came into view, covered in long vines of the same flowers. Kate pushed through the curtain of flowers and beheld a large spiral labyrinth before her, identical green bushes precisely trimmed. The fragrance of the flowers was too enticing to ignore, and Kate turned around one last time to smell the magnificent flowers. Instead, she felt a soft petal on her face as the flowers strained towards her, and rubbed her face like kittens. She giggled and automatically looked down for the black cat who appeared at her feet as if by magic. She bent down to pet the smooth, long black fur. "Well, Miss Luna, you look pretty good for a cat your age."

"You look well too. They've missed you." Miss Luna flicked her fluffy tail towards the flowers that strained towards her.

Kate pulled them into her embrace as they covered her face in flower kisses. She turned back towards Miss Luna.

"I remember these flowers, and talking with you as we walked through the maze."

"Yes, I rather liked our talks and was quite fond of you. It's been a long time and we all missed you, as you can tell," Miss Luna said, flicking her tail once more towards the flowers still straining to touch Kate. She laughed and embraced them one last time to their delight. After a moment Kate let go and turned towards the maze. "Shall we walk it, Miss Luna? For old times' sake? I find that I could use one of our talks very badly right now."

"What's troubling you?"

"This is all real, isn't it?" Kate bit her thumbnail and walked further down the path.

"It is, I can assure you." Miss Luna walked next to Kate, tail held high.

"Then dimensions are real, and so are other worlds."

"Yes."

"It just makes me feel a bit like I'm losing my mind. Other dimensions? Talking cats? That is not normal." Kate glanced down at Miss Luna.

"Normal is relative," the black cat replied with a sniff. "You know deep down what the truth is."

Kate's feet faltered. She did know but hadn't wanted to accept it until now.

"I guess I just need to accept there are other worlds out there."

"Finally!" Miss Luna replied with a huff. "Things are starting to happen, and I was afraid you wouldn't be ready."

"What things?" Kate asked, but Miss Luna disappeared through the underbrush, leaving her alone.

She walked on through the maze, hands in her pockets, lost in her thoughts when she noticed the wind pick up. Within moments it whipped through the bushes and tugged hard on her hair and clothes as the sky turned black and ominous. She shivered and turned her feet around to retrace her steps back to the house. Her hair blew across her eyes and Kate stumbled into the bushes and felt them grow and twist in her hands. She pulled her hair back enough to see all the bushes stretch over her, twisted and sinister in the encroaching darkness. Kate broke into a jog and encountered a dead end. Wait, there were no dead ends in here! She remembered how much she loved that. There was no fear that she would ever get lost in it because there were no dead ends, until you reached the center of the circle.

She tried to push through the wall of bushes only to have them grip her in a tight embrace. Blood dripped down her scratched arms and panic set it. She pulled and twisted until she was free, and ran, unsure of which way was out.

The sky broke open and rain pelted her skin. The ground beneath her turned to slick mud and Kate fell, got up, and fell again, unable to gain traction. She screamed for help, but the wind snatched the words away. She spun around in a circle looking for a way out, but the bushes grabbed her again, tighter this time.

A blazing white light lit up the sky above her and a hole slowly opened where the light had been to reveal a green face covered in oozing sores with pointy teeth and sharp tusks. It spotted Kate, and its eyes widened then narrowed.

"A Jones," it hissed as the hole widened enough for the monster's muscular body to push through and jump to the ground. The ground shook under its powerful legs, and the branches loosened just enough for her to dart through the underbrush.

Fear gripped her heart and her mind raced as she scrambled through a break in the bushes and pelted away. What *was* this thing and how did it know her? She didn't have a chance of outrunning it; its legs were too powerful. She couldn't fight it, but could she hurt it enough to find a hiding place?

The creature's shriek of rage bellowed through the night and nearly made Kate's knees buckle but she raced on. It followed and ripped bushes out of the ground as easy as a human plucking out a tiny weed in its pursuit of Kate.

"You can't hope to win, descendant of Jones. I will find you."

Kate ducked behind a stand of trees. *Think, Kate, think. What can hurt this thing?* Kate desperately wracked her brain, but nothing came up. There was nothing in this world that could help her. That thing was huge and powerful, and she wasn't strong enough to fight it without any weapons. She didn't even know if there were weapons at the house and didn't dare try to get back there. Even if there were weapons at the house, she wasn't sure they would do anything against its tough leathery skin.

Suddenly Kate lurched forward as the earth erupted behind her. She caught her balance and took off, dodging the tree the monster easily tossed her way. She risked a look behind her to see it lumbering after her, full of confidence in the outcome, like a cat playing with its prey, only stronger and uglier.

"You cannot possibly hope to outrun me on those weak human legs. You will lose in the end."

She knew it was right. Even now her lungs burned and a cramp seized her side, but she ran on. She spotted the kissing flower arbor tunnel and veered towards it. Those flowers. There was something about them. What was it? Miss Luna's voice filled her head as a memory took shape.

"It's a small, delicate flower now because it likes you, but things would be different if they felt threatened. They're amazing at protecting themselves."

"How?" her young self asked, and Miss Luna explained.

That was it! With renewed strength Kate pushed herself and ran with everything she had through the tunnel, collapsing to the ground at the other end. She prayed her memory was true because she couldn't run anymore.

Seconds later the creature came into view. It eyed the exhausted Kate and with a triumphant roar, ripped the flowers out and tried to toss them aside. Its roar broke off and it looked incredulous as the flowers rapidly grew in size. The vines wrapped themselves around it in a tight embrace as the creature first shrugged, then struggled as the vines tightened. It screamed in rage, but the flowers reared up, and blew their poison pollen in its face.

The creature stopped struggling and blinked in confusion a few times. "What is this? What is this?"

Tiny voices shouted a tiny war cry as Dasme and Flora appeared in front of Kate carrying the tiny staff.

"What are you doing? You'll get hurt!" Kate yelled.

"Have no fear, Kate! Are you ready, Flora?"

"Ready, Dasme," Flora shouted.

Dasme and Flora anchored the staff into the ground, pointed it directly at the creature, and pulled the lever. A giant ray of light burst from the tip of the staff, hitting the creature in the chest, hurtling it backwards through the portal in the sky as it shut with a bang.

Everything was still for a moment before Kate crawled over to Dasme and Flora, scooped them up, and planted kisses on both their noses.

"Madame, if you please, unhand me." Dasme struggled against Kate's embrace. Kate laughed and put them both down.

"I'm sorry, but thank you!!! Thank you!! You saved me."

"Well, we helped. We couldn't have hit it if you hadn't subdued it with the flowers. Brilliant idea by the way," Flora responded.

Kate looked up as the sky cleared and the sun came out. She could almost believe it had never happened, except for the green carnage strewn about the yard. Her face fell and she found the strength to stumble over to the pile of flowers, small again, wilted on the ground. They mewled softy and nudged Kate's hand.

"No, no, no, you can't die. Please don't die," she said as tears spilled down her face.

Mr. H appeared out of nowhere at her elbow.

"Here, Miss, let's get them into the greenhouse. I think I can save some of them."

They gingerly picked up the flowers and carried them to the greenhouse where pots and dirt waited. They worked in silence and quickly got the flowers into their new homes.

"A bit of water, a bit of food, a bit of music, and a bit of love. They'll be good as new in a few weeks, Miss, you'll see."

Kate looked at the perked-up flowers and had no doubt Mr. H was right. She leaned in for more flower kisses as she whispered what brave little flowers they were and straightened up.

"Are you guys OK?" Kate asked Flora and Dasme.

"Yes, we're fine. We'll help Mr. H with the flowers if he doesn't mind. Everyone in the garden is quite fond of them."

Kate nodded then strode towards the house, determined to get answers.

12) Mrs. B and Kate

Kate threw open the kitchen door to see Mrs. B bustling about the kitchen as if nothing had transpired. A spark of anger roared into a flame and consumed her body. Hadn't she noticed Kate fighting for her life out there, or didn't she care? Had she been too busy baking to notice? Hot tears threatened to spill over and she shouted at Mrs. B over the rush in her ears. Mrs. B whirled around and Kate was surprised to see her red rimmed eyes and ruddy cheeks, as if she had been crying. Her eyes flashed at Kate before she took a deep breath and gestured towards the kitchen table. Kate fell into a chair, shook her head, and tried to clear the noise as her teeth chattered. A moment later Mrs. B draped a blanket over Kate's shoulders, and a cup of hot tea had been placed in her hands. Grateful, Kate wrapped her fingers around the cup for warmth.

They sat in silence until Kate could hear again.

"What was that?" Kate asked.

"The shock hit you dear." Mrs. B wrapped her hands around Kate's on the mug and met her gaze. "I tried to help you, but the house,"—Mrs. B threw a look of disgust up to the ceiling — "wouldn't let me out. I tried every door and window, even tried breaking a few but it wouldn't budge. I'm so sorry Kate. I knew you needed help, and I wasn't able to be there for you."

Kate brought the cup to her lips. "Maybe the house had its reasons. Honestly it might have been worse if I had you there to worry about." Kate pictured Mrs. B going up against the creature with nothing but a rolling pin and smiled. She probably would have sent it back by sheer will. Her smile faltered.

"I had a dream. In it Aunt Esme warned me that he was coming and not to let him get the journal. This can't be a coincidence, can it? But what would that thing want with Aunt Esme's stories?" Kate's hands shook, and she lowered the cup to the table.

Mrs. B pushed a plate of lemon cookies closer to Kate. "It'll help with the shock."

Kate reached for a cookie and nibbled the soft edges as tartness and sweetness flooded her mouth.

"If your aunt warned you not to let him get the journal, there must be something important in it. Have you come across anything?"

"Nothing!" Kate replied morosely. "What happened to Aunt Esme? Where did she go?" Kate asked, afraid of the answer.

"I wish I knew. She never told me where she was going when she traveled and it wasn't unusual for her to be gone months at a time. But this…this is the longest she's been away, and then you showed up, which isn't a coincidence."

Kate blurted out, "Do you think she's alive?"

"I do. Your aunt's resourceful and smart." Mrs. B smiled at Kate. "You're more like her than you realize." Mrs. B paused for a moment before she met and held Kate's gaze. "I think you're the key to finding your aunt."

"What do you mean?" Kate shook her head in confusion.

"I think you have some memories or knowledge locked up." Mrs. B pointed at Kate's head. "Something that could tell us how to help her." Mrs. B reached out and grasped Kate's hand.

"How can I possibly know that? I haven't seen her in years. You must be wrong. Isn't there anyone else who can help?" Kate looked around the kitchen as if for answers.

"Her blood runs through your veins. Her abilities may be your abilities—" Kate started at that but Mrs. B continued. "She may have shown you something that summer, something you've blocked for some reason."

Her blood runs through your veins. Her abilities may be your abilities. Kate pondered the significance of those words. Was it really so far-fetched? After everything that had happened? Kate knew it wasn't, but the burden of being her aunt's salvation was a heavy load.

"How do I remember? Can't someone just *tell* me?" Kate dropped her head down onto the table and groaned.

"I wish it could be that easy. Look, you've made a start by accepting this is real but I think it'll help if you confront the old wounds to your heart. The ones caused by your aunt. That might make this process easier."

"I don't have any old wounds. If I did, I would know—trust me. I have enough from my mom," Kate stated and took another bite of the pillowy soft cookie.

"It's there, I can sense it. You need to figure out what they are in order to let go and see things clearly."

She mulled over Mrs. B's words and knew she was right. She dredged up all her memories of Aunt Esme, birthdays and Christmases and other random holidays. She turned them over and examined them from an adult perspective and was startled to feel the pain she had pushed down for so long.

"I didn't . . . I mean I wasn't aware how hurt I was?" Kate replied, overcome at the intense emotions that bubbled up. "I think we'd grown close that summer, and after my mom came and got me, nothing, except visits on birthdays and holidays. I loved seeing her, but it hurt. I thought she didn't love me as much as I loved her."

"Oh, poppet, she loved you so, so much," Mrs. B uttered.

"If she loved me so much, why did she stay away? Why didn't she ask me to stay here again?" Kate asked.

"Maybe she did. Would your mom have told you if she had?" Mrs. B searched Kate's face.

Kate sighed. Of course, her mom wouldn't have told her. Her mom liked her aunt as much as she liked the house.

"Being an adult is complicated, Kate, which you can see now. Think back to how your aunt was treated when she did visit."

"I loved when she visited and would cry when she left. I could never understand why my mom got so mad when she showed up. Aunt Esme and my mom would fight every time until she showed up less and less." Kate was startled by the tears streaming down her face as she finally allowed herself to feel the pain of losing her aunt, long before she went missing.

Mrs. B handed her a tissue from her apron. "So maybe it wasn't about not loving you enough and more about loving her sister too much."

"Maybe," Kate replied as relief swept through her. Her aunt did love her and tried to be there for her. Now she needed to be there for Aunt Esme. She stood up and handed Mrs. B the blanket. "I'm going home to shower, collect some clothes, and then I'll be back. I need to read more of her journal. Maybe there's something in it to help Aunt Esme. Either way, I need to be here."

Mrs. B nodded. "I'll make up your old room. Welcome home, Kate."

13) Best Friends

Kate slipped through the front door of the apartment hoping to get into the shower before Maggie saw her. She hadn't thought that part through very well. Chalk it up to exhaustion after fighting a massive interdimensional monster. She almost made it to the bathroom when Maggie came barging out of her room and stopped as she stared at Kate in shock.

"What happened to you?"

Kate looked down at her mud-encrusted clothes, shirt torn from the bushes, dried blood caked on her arms, and fought back hot tears.

"Kate, what happened out there?" Maggie demanded.

"Nothing. I got caught in a thunderstorm and slipped in mud."

"You do not look like that from 'slipping' in some mud. What's going on with you? You've been acting secretive lately and we don't keep secrets from each other, ever, remember?"

"You wouldn't understand," Kate said. If she barely understood it, how could she ask Maggie to?

"What exactly wouldn't I understand? What in the world is there that you can't tell your best friend?" Maggie's eyes bored into Kate's. "I'm worried about you. You aren't sleeping—don't think I didn't notice those bags under your eyes. Your mom, whom you've been avoiding, has been blowing up my phone. You haven't been painting except for a couple pieces. You keep disappearing into that house. AND you're avoiding me and my texts."

"It's complicated," Kate whispered. She desperately wanted to pour everything out to her best friend but stopped herself. How would that sound? Not to mention would it put her best friend in danger from that creature?

"That's the difference. I open up and tell you everything, and you keep everything closed in. That's not how friendships work. You don't have to go through this alone. I'm here for you, but you're being selfish. You keep everything bottled up so you don't have to feel uncomfortable talking about your emotions."

"That's unfair, Mags. I'm trying to protect you," Kate shouted as she turned and stepped into the bathroom so she wouldn't have to face Maggie.

"From what?" Maggie demanded.

"I can't tell you," Kate mumbled as she started the shower.

"Of course, you can't. Cuz everything in your life lately is some big dark secret." Maggie looked down at her phone. "I'm late for a meeting. We can talk about this later."

"I won't be here. I'm staying at my aunt's for a few days to sort things out." Kate cringed at how that sounded but knew there was no other way. If she wanted answers she had to stay where it all began and be ready if that thing came through again. Although, how she would be ready, she was still working out.

"You know what, I can't with you right now. I am woman enough to say I am angry and hurt that you feel you can't trust me, but you can't run away forever. We have to deal with this if you truly value our friendship."

"I do," Kate replied as steam filled the small enclosure and surrounded them.

"Then show it and let me in," Maggie pleaded.

"I . . . can't," Kate replied, shoulders slumped. She loved her best friend too much to dump all this on her. Plus, would she even believe her? Dimensions? Doors? Other planets? She barely believed it herself. If she hadn't battled a green monster, she wasn't sure she would have believed it all.

"UGH. I can't either." Maggie stormed out of the house. Kate jumped as the front door slammed, and she fought back tears. She was doing it to protect Mags. Maybe one day she would tell her but for now, she needed to focus on Aunt Esme and finding something that would lead to her aunt's whereabouts. And if she did find something, what would she be able to do about it? Kate sighed. She would figure that out when she got to that point. For now, a hot shower called to her.

The sound of the alarm jarred Kate out of sleep the next morning. Her muscles screamed as she reached out to shut it off. Apparently battling a green monster did a number on a body. Exhausted, she had collapsed into bed as soon as she got back to the house.

A few moments later Kate was in the kitchen where breakfast had been laid out. Kate's stomach rumbled as the smell of freshly baked biscuits wafted from the tray. She grabbed a warm biscuit, slathered it with fresh butter and honey, and gobbled it down. Honey dripped down her hand and she savored the taste as she licked it off. Food had never tasted this good before. Something about Mrs. B's cooking made even the simple things taste like the best she had ever eaten. After four biscuits, all slathered with copious amounts of butter and honey, and a giant bowl of berries, her stomach was finally satisfied when someone struck the front door over and over. The pounding echoed through the house as someone demanded attention.

Kate's first panicked thought was that the creature was back, but reason gave way. There was no way it would knock on the door and wait to be let in. Still, trepidation filled her as she inched her way closer to the front door, before she peered out and saw Maggie standing there, legs spread, hands on hips with a determined look on her face.

"Dammit, Kate, I know you're in there!" Maggie pounded the door again just as Kate flung the door open.

"You can stop trying to break the door down. What are you doing here?"

"Being a good best friend, which is more than I can say for you. Your mom called me. She's trying to see if she needs to plan an intervention for you. I assured her that all is well and you were just busy painting for the art show that I thought was supposed to happen. Which I don't even know if you're doing anymore because you haven't talked to me! Girl, what is going on with you? Don't give me that look. I'm your best friend and I'm not letting you push me away. Oh, AND your mom wants me to report back on your every move. Does she even know me? Pshh. But I did buy you a few days. So, start talking so we can communicate like adults and the best friends that we are."

Kate stood staring at her best friend and had never loved her more than she did right at that moment. She nodded and gestured for Maggie to come in. It was time to tell her everything and see what happened. She needed her best friend.

Kate slumped back against the study chair, exhausted from talking. She looked at Maggie who remained silent and pensive.

"Say something, Maggie."

"I'm trying to find the right words," Maggie replied, as she absently stroked Miss Luna, curled up in her lap.

"You can start by saying you believe me."

"I believe *you* believe the story you told me," Maggie said.

"That's a shit answer. You wanted me to tell you everything and I did just that."

"Yeah, but I was expecting you to be grappling with some family drama, not be thrown into an episode of *Stranger Things*. It's just a lot to take in. What about your mom?"

"What about her?" Kate asked, confused.

"Have you talked to her? Asked her about any of this? From what you've said she grew up in this house and may know what's going on or where to look for your aunt."

"She wouldn't. She's always refused to talk about this house, my aunt, or anyone else in my family. She'd freak out if she knew I was here, and who knows what she would do. Ban me from returning? Keep me locked up in her house? I don't want to chance it."

"OK. Let's say I believe this is all real. How can you help your aunt if you don't know if she's even alive or where she's at? You haven't traveled to other dimensions, have you?"

"I don't think so. At least, none that I remember, which is why I need to remember that summer! What if I knew how to travel or spot doors?" Kate sat up in excitement.

"You'd remember that, wouldn't you?" Maggie asked gently. "That seems like a very big thing to remember."

"So you believe me?"

"Kate, we've been best friends since the fourth grade, and we've always looked out for each other; I'm not about to stop now. You believe this is happening, which is all that matters right now."

"How nice," Miss Luna said from Maggie's lap.

Maggie bolted upright from the chair and flung Miss Luna to the ground.

"What . . . was . . . that?" Maggie demanded, eyes wide.

"No need to be rude about it. I thought we were hitting it off splendidly." Miss Luna sat, licked a paw, and smoothed the fur on her ear.

"Maggie, meet Miss Luna. Miss Luna, meet my best friend, Maggie."

Kate laid a hand on Maggie's arm and tried to pull her back into her seat.

"How do you do?" Miss Luna asked.

"Oh Lord, no no no no. A cat did not just ask me, 'how do I do.'" Magge's nostrils flared. "It has to be this house. Gas coming from a leak, or from the vents like that murder castle hotel."

"This isn't like that at all," Kate said.

"Then how do you explain a talking cat?" Maggie asked, voice raised a few octaves.

Kate turned towards Miss Luna and cocked her head. "Care to answer?"

"I assumed this shape when I came to this dimension from my own."

"Like a shapeshifter? Can you change into anything else?" Kate asked, intrigued.

"I could, but it takes a tremendous amount of energy, and there's never been any need. Honestly, I'm not sure I would have the energy to change back to this form and I've grown rather fond of being Miss Luna."

"See, there's your answer," Kate replied. "Now if you would just sit down . . ."

"And catch the crazy that is obviously going around? This CANNOT be real Kate."

"Stop. I know this is a lot to take in. I was where you were not that long ago and I'm asking you to believe me, and trust that this is real. It's not a hallucination, and it's not mental health issues; this is as real as you and me standing here right now. Now breathe. Remember the yoga class you made me take?'

"Not really," Maggie said,

"That's because you missed half the class flirting with Mr. Abs at the front desk."

Maggie tilted her head and pursed her lips. "Now *him* I remember. He never did ask me out."

"But you did learn some breathing techniques, remember?" Kate prompted.

"Honestly, no, now you have me rethinking Mr. Abs."

"Maggie, focus!" Kate said.

"Yes, I know how to breathe." Maggie relaxed into the chair but jumped up immediately and shrieked. "What is that?" she asked with a shaky finger at Chirp who clung to the back of the chair.

"Chirp," Kate replied.

"I have officially heard it all."

"Are you OK?"

"Does it look like I'm OK? My best friend tells me a story about dimensions and monsters, a cat asked me how I was, and now you have a pet thing," Maggie gestured erratically at Chirp, "you named Chirp."

At that exact moment, Chirp tilted its head quizzically, and chirped at Maggie. They both burst into laughter, unable to stop, until they collapsed, arms hugging their sides, tears streaming down their faces. After a while their laughter tapered off, and they sat up.

"Well I guess I should go home and get some clothes. What?" Maggie asked at Kate's stunned look. "You don't think I'm leaving you to handle this on your own, do you? Do you not know your best friend?"

Kate threw her arms around her best friend in relief. She did think she had to do this alone, but she realized she had people she loved to help her. Maggie, Mrs. B, Miss Luna, Chirp, Mr. H. Her heart swelled and she finally felt capable of handling whatever came their way.

14) Deprama 1

Kate sank back into the chair and opened the journal. *Please Aunt Esme, let me find something, anything, to help you.* Again, words ran off the page and swirled around the room. She felt the now familiar vertigo as her awareness tumbled into Aunt Esme's memory.

"Do you have everything you need?" Aslame questioned as we stood before the door.

I nodded and pulled a few things out of my travel bag. One was a tiny earbud I placed in my ear, which accompanied a small bird suspended on a barely perceptible filament. I wrapped the filament around my throat twice and let the bird rest on my vocal cords. The technology was programmed with thousands of languages from across dimensions so I should be able to understand whatever was said to me, and whoever I spoke to would hear their language being spoken back.

I scanned the door with another device I pulled from my bag and read the readout. No signs of any thermal readings within a one-mile radius, so I would be safe going through. Negative ten degrees. Probably why there were no heat signals. I sighed. Why couldn't it have been a tropical island? Why was it always a frigid cold planet? At least I already had on thermals—and not just any regular thermals.

These had tiny wires woven into the fabric to keep the skin covered at a consistent temperature, to either warm me up or cool me down. The last thing I checked was the oxygen: 19.2 percent. Not terrible, but I would need a bit of help which came in the form of another amazing piece of technology from the Peradite's, which I clipped to the inside of my nostrils. Advanced nanotechnology that, when activated, would heat up the microscopic crystals and release the oxygen being held in the crystals which also absorbed any harmful gasses. Eons ahead of our time.

I threw my bag over my shoulder and tucked it under my cloak. "I'll find them and bring them back." I promised.

"M'ra has faith in you, Merelda. We all do."

I pulled my goggles over my eyes, and without a glance back, stepped through the door.

The first thing I noticed was the bitter cold as it wrapped me in its icy embrace like a lost lover, its frozen tendrils probing for exposed skin to sting and slap. I pulled my cloak tighter and shivered. Even with my protective clothing I would need to find shelter fairly quickly.

The second thing I noticed was the total darkness, utter and complete, from the sky devoid of any stars or moons, to the ground where my feet should have been. The world spun as the darkness consumed me and I could no longer tell up from down. I squeezed my eyes shut against the spinning. I pushed a button on my goggles and waited for the world to stabilize. Precious seconds passed before I pried open my eyes and looked around at emptiness.

Now, these goggles were the top of the line on Denook, which usually meant when I used the night vision that it looked just like day would. Except here. Here everything still looked like dusk. I saw outlines of tall, dark, faceless buildings with no apparent windows or doors and empty, abandoned streets. While this made it more difficult to see, it was still better than the complete blackness. I burrowed down into my cloak and strode down the empty street towards a building. I studied it for any way in and ran my hands over its seamless surface for any small crack, but the cold forced me to move.

I jogged down street after street, trying to find any way in, until my vision blurred from tears, and I feared for my appendages. I sped up and tore around a corner and froze before instinct took over and I scrambled back to safety. A rookie mistake but I blamed it on this horrid planet. I wiped my eyes and risked a look to assess the creatures that blocked the street.

There were four of them, with large, thick skin littered with cracks and wrinkles, like mud that's baked in the sun too long, and tufts of hair sprouting sporadically over their large bodies. Elongated faces held double rows of sharp teeth, and two sets of eyes locked on their prize they had surrounded. One held a bright lantern that illuminated the area around them.

I hugged the walls and crept forward until I was close enough for the translator to detect the dialect as the creatures bobbed and wove around their prey.

"Pram will love this one. Strong for the fights. He'll be pleased with us."

"Yess, he will be pleased. Fair game on the ssurface, you know that."

A creature stood confidently in the center and cast a scornful look on the thick-skinned creatures. It stood just as tall but had razor sharp horns and was covered in shaggy black fur with massive hands that could easily crush a boulder. Laughter erupted from its mouth.

"Pram does not want to mess with a Grangula, and you know it, Taporrs."

The Taporrs bobbed their heads, and glanced at each other

uneasily, unsure if the Grangula was telling the truth. It seemed they didn't want to risk Pram's displeasure.

"Try to come at me and you'll all end up dead. Besides there's easier prey behind you." Sixteen sets of eyes turned towards me in unison, which is when the Grangula sauntered away.

"What is it?"

"I've never seen anything like it."

"Pram will be pleassssed with this one."

"It looks sssoft. Maybe it tastess good."

"Maybe we see and don't tell Pram."

The creatures lumbered towards me, but I had already taken off. My mind raced with questions. How had that creature seen past my cloak? While it didn't make me invisible, it gave the strong suggestion that I wasn't worth looking at. It should have worked here unless the creature was highly observant and had pierced the suggestion. Whatever it was, the suggestion had been broken and the Taporrs could now see me. My options at this point dwindled, which put me in a precarious position to say the least. I couldn't go back through the door and risk the Taporrs following me into Trilesk, and I couldn't find a way into the buildings. I risked a glance over my shoulder, and the taporrs trudged behind with a steady gait. They didn't seem too concerned that I would get away. And why would they? The cold would slow me down eventually and they knew the terrain of the city.

I needed to catch my breath, so I ducked behind a building just as a large vehicle careened around the corner and slammed on its brakes. Three short squat individuals with thick arms jumped out of the front, walked over to the wall, and pounded. A door slid open seamlessly and a haggard-looking vulture woman eyed them. That certainly explained why I couldn't find any doors to get in.

"You're late." Her gravely voice betrayed her irritation.

"He's feisty. We had to pull over twice to tank him, and he still woke up. We can't do a third dose, so you'll need help getting him."

The woman grimaced then smiled slyly as the Taporrs came into view.

"You four!" she shrieked. "Get over here and help. Pram wants this one to fight tomorrow."

"We're hunting a creature for Pram's collection."

"Do you want to be the one to tell Pram you thought finding something for his zoo took precedence over one of his fighters?"

The creatures swayed back and forth in agitation.

"No, no, no, we'll help get the fighter in. The fighter is much more important. We would never ssay no to one of Pram's fighters."

"That's what I thought. Now get him in here quickly. I hate this cold."

The squat creatures grabbed long prongs that ended in flat circles while the Taporrs circled the back of the truck. One of the squatters hit a band on his wrist and the back opened. A large, muscular beast stood, arms and legs shackled to the sides and bottom of the truck. It snorted smoke out of its flared nostrils and buckled the floor as it stomped its flat feet in one last attempt to free itself.

"You know what happens if you misbehave, Fey," the squatters threatened as they approached the back of the van, sparks flying from the end of their prongs.

The creature's head flailed back, and a roar of anguish and rage erupted from his mouth. I stayed still and willed them to hurry but I was torn. I needed to get inside as quickly as possible, yet I wanted this poor creature to fight and escape whatever life and atrocities awaited him here.

The squatters jabbed the creature, and it arched its back as the electricity jolted through him. Its mouth foamed and it fought to stay conscious.

"Let's get him to his cage quickly. I have enough to do tonight without babysitting detail," the vulture woman screeched. The squatters systematically unlocked the chains holding Fey down, and stepped back as a Taporr each took a limb, and carried Fey in, face down. I darted across the street behind the truck as clinks of what I presumed was money exchanged hands from the front of the transport truck.

The vulture woman turned and followed the Taporrs into the building and I barely made it through to the darkened hallway before the door slid closed. I rubbed my limbs as fire coursed over my skin and waited until their voices faded. I crept down a hall and after a few hundred feet, small rooms appeared on either side. I peered into one, and saw it had no windows, with only a small bucket and filthy hay piled in a corner. It reeked of urine, sweat, terror, and other horrible smells I could not name. Further down I saw prisoners, one per room, gaunt and filthy but the eerie silence affected me the most. They all had vacant stares, and the air of abject hopelessness and misery was heavy as I passed. I knew I could do nothing to help them today and that tore at my soul. I quickened my pace but didn't seem to gain any distance and I feared this was one of those nightmares where the hall just grew and grew, no matter how fast you ran. Eventually I did approach the end of the hall, and I slowed as I heard voices.

"That last one was tough."

"Some days are like that. You have to give Progos what they came for, but you have to be careful that they don't die too soon. The Progos don't like that. They want you to take your time so they can savor every scream. If they die too soon, we have to get another one and you know we're supposed to limit it to one a day, otherwise we run out and it's hard to get more. Don't be too hard on yourself. You're still learning, and they did get quite a show before it died so maybe they won't complain."

"What if they do?"

"Only the boss knows what'll happen to you."

I peered around the corner and saw a pair of creatures, tall and spindly, like stick figures a child would draw. They had long arms that dragged on the ground, and a head with a single large eye in the center over a large mouth. Above their singular eye was a black crystal embedded in its head, one deepest of black, the other lightest of grey. Rage threatened to take over and I quelled the murderous urge to snap the creatures in two—which, while it may have been extremely satisfying, would have alerted others to my presence—and waited for them to move down the passage. I had seen much in my travels, and I considered myself a strong individual, but it still never dulled the pain of seeing innocents not only suffer but suffer needlessly and horrifically for the pleasure of others. I would never be able to understand that type of depravity and hoped I never would.

Their footsteps faded and I hurried through the chamber, eyes focused on the floor until I stood before two passageways, where one led down and the other led upwards. After a quick look down the deserted hall I strode forward and hoped the cloak still worked. Loud noises from behind a pair of double doors stopped me and I pushed one in just enough to peer through. It looked like a kitchen with various creatures at different stations. Some stirred pots, some chopped giant tubers, some scurried away with trays, and a giant blob with tiny eyes sat in the center and yelled orders. Crystals were also embedded in these creatures' heads, but they ranged from deepest amethyst to palest lavender.

I closed the door and tucked the crystal mystery into the back corner of my mind. I needed to get out of the lower levels if I had any chance of finding Miswala and Kokshai and knew they wouldn't be kept with the other prisoners. The Depramese would not have planned such an elaborate kidnapping if they didn't want Miswala and Kokshai for specific reasons, which meant they were valuable. Valuable belongings were not sent to the dungeons; they were kept in cages close to their owners. Which also meant they were most likely being held on the upper floors since that's where the powerful and rich stayed—some things were universal—and I couldn't see this being orchestrated by a middle man. I followed the corridor down for some time until I came upon a bank of what I hoped were elevators and slipped in. My luck held out as there was no one on the elevators—and there had been no one in the halls—and I hit a symbol that I thought might be the middle floors. My nerves were taut and I hoped there would be more people on the middle floors. You would think empty was good but halls with one or two made it easier for someone to penetrate my cloak and notice me which usually led to questions I was unwilling or unable to answer. Yes, I much preferred blending in than standing out.

And why didn't I go up to the top floors immediately? Security would be tighter, for one, and make it difficult to gather information, which I needed, and to do that I needed to find a place where talk flowed more freely and I could move about.

The elevators came to a soft stop and opened. I stepped out into the throngs and matched their leisurely stroll down the wide corridors. Out of the corner of my eyes I noticed these creatures were sans embedded crystals but wore theirs as adornments on pins, rings, atop canes and reeked of privilege. Every few hundred feet, some would peel off and enter the rotunda's dotting the hallways. I glanced in each one as I passed—gambling, restaurants, fighting—and noticed again the creatures that worked the areas had different colored crystals embedded in their heads. I followed behind a voluminous dress as it converged on a large room with packed seats surrounding a stage hidden by heavy curtains. I found an empty one in the back and settled in. Something told me to stay, and I always listen.

Music began to play, and the curtain was drawn to reveal a young woman, with black hair and a sapphire blue jewel the same shade as her eyes. Clatter fell away as her sultry smooth voice flowed through the room and wrapped its silkiness around each patron. They sat immobilized and rapt through song after song. I swear she could have had them sit there till the end of time, without food or drink, just to hear her voice.

The lights dimmed and the room held their breath in anticipation. Most of the band put down their instruments except for one, who, when combined with the singer's voice, wove a forlorn tapestry of such longing that it left the room in tears, even if most did not understand the words. Even I was not immune as the words provoked images of home.

I yearn for the feel of bare feet on grass, I yearn for the warmth of the sun,
I yearn for the gentle wind on my cheeks, I cry and I yearn for home,
I yearn for the water, so deep and blue, I yearn for the clouds overhead,
I yearn for the trees, so tall and green, I cry and I yearn for home,
There must be more than this life I know, there must be a way out,
There must be a door I cannot see as I cry and I yearn for home.

The last note hung in the air and everyone held their breath, as if it would break. Silence ensued for a moment and then and then everyone leapt to their feet and stomped as the room roared their approval for their favorite singer. The girl smiled and slipped off the stage before anyone could approach her as the band changed pace and a dance floor was cleared and quickly filled. I pulled my cloak close and darted after as my instinct urged me to follow. We went down corridor after corridor, where every privileged person she encountered gushed their love for her before they backed off with a quick glance over their shoulder. These people obviously adored her but held back from accosting her. Interesting. She strode down an empty hall and stopped before a door and entered a room. Seeing my chance, I lunged forward and jammed my foot into the door before it closed and slipped in.

"What are you doing? How dare you enter my private chamber. Do you know what Pram will do to you for this?" The girl's face grew red as her eyes narrowed and her voice rose.

I didn't answer but instead took off my goggles and faced her as the color drained from her face. She stumbled against the wall as if she had been hit.

"This is impossible. All my people are dead. What are you? Were you sent by Pram? You don't have a crystal, so you must be a Progo and Progos aren't allowed in my room. Pram will have your head for this!"

"I'm not a Progo and I can assure you all your people aren't dead. In fact there's an entire planet of your people who live freely."

"I don't believe you. You must be lying. What do you want?"

"I want my friends who were kidnapped and brought here, and I have a feeling you can help me."

"No one can help them, and you should pray to whatever god you think exists that they're already dead."

15) Deprama 2

She took a few steps down into a living room and collapsed on the couch.

"Why would I pray for their death?"

"The alternative's much worse. This is the place where nightmares are born," her voice shook as her shoulders trembled. She eyed me up and down as I stepped down into the room.

"I was always told I was the last of my kind."

"You were told wrong. Is there anyone else here?" I gestured towards the back rooms.

"You're welcome to look," she said and looked bored, but I didn't trust her. I gestured for her to go first and checked to make sure all the rooms were empty before coming back to the living room.

"What's your name?" I asked.

"Claraseve," she said and settled back into the couch.

"Well, Claraseve, I'd like to exchange information." Claraseve's eyes narrowed, and I continued, "I need information about this city, and it seems like I can provide you with some information about your origins. Do we have a deal?"

Claraseve studied me for a moment then nodded her head.

"Tell me about Pram," I began.

Claraseve got up and poured herself a drink. She gestured to the small table that held what I assumed was liquor and I declined. She sat back down and swirled the drink, lost in thought, before she answered.

"Deprama is a playground for the richest, most powerful, most sadistic beings you will ever come across. This is where they come to live out their fantasies, whatever they may be, and do whatever they please. Progos pay a steep price to be here and come from across all the galaxies."

"And Pram?" I prompted.

"Pram runs this place."

I felt her reluctance and changed the subject, determined to circle back to Pram again.

"How did you get here so far from Earth?"

"Is that what you call where we're from? It's a pretty name. I don't know how we got here; we've just always been here. My muma taught me that song when I was little. She was a singer and the Progos adored her, which is the only reason she was able to keep me. She hid the pregnancy from Pram and when he found out after she gave birth, she threatened to drink acid if they tried to take me. I'm not sure why Pram let her have me. Maybe he was having a good day. Or maybe the uproar if the Progos lost their beloved singer made him back off. Whatever the reason, she kept me safe until the day she died when I was six. The only reason I was spared again after her death was because I showed promise as a singer. I worked and ranked up over the years . . ."

"Ranked up?" I interrupted as she knocked back her drink and got up for another.

"There's a ranking system amongst the vasels. The better your work, the more you're ranked up, which earns you a darker crystal and more privilege. Higher-ranked vasels are kept in better rooms, get better food, and we're not expected to work our fingers to the bone like the lower vasels. It's the most we can ever expect in this life." Bitterness tinged her words.

"What about escaping? Surely others have tried and made it out."

Claraseve threw a scornful look at me. "If a vasel tried to escape they would be found and relegated to the torture chambers. These crystals mark us as Pram's property and can't be removed. If someone does manage to escape, they're almost always brought back and thrown in the dungeons." Claraseve shuddered. "No one would harbor an escaped vasel and risk crossing Pram. He holds the key to the Progos' immortality, an elixir that stops aging and keeps them young for as long as they take the serum. For a hefty price, of course. So you see, it's useless to try to escape."

"Would you know where they kept valuable prisoners by chance?" I asked, but Claraseve held my gaze and refused to answer.

I pulled my sleeve up to reveal a thin, silver, inconspicuous bracelet.

"What's that?" Claraseve eyes narrowed.

"Maybe you'll be more willing to tell me what I need to know after seeing this. I replied and pushed a small button on the bracelet.

Claraseve gasped as images and videos filled the room.

"What is this?"

"Memories. More specifically my memories, my most treasured ones. This one was taken at the beach." I pointed to an image of me smiling into the camera, one hand holding a straw hat on my head as the wind tried to snatch it off. The sun behind me was low in the sky as the surf crept up the sand.

"The Northern Lights." I pointed to another picture of a night sky streaked with greens and purples.

"The Redwood Forest." Two tiny people dwarfed against a massive tree ten of us couldn't have encircled.

Eyes wide, mouth open, Claraseve spun around as her eyes devoured the images.

"What's that one?" Claraseve pointed to a picture of a young child, smiling into the camera, on roller skates with scraped knees.

"My niece, who's my world."

I pushed the button again and dispelled the images back to my bracelet. Claraseve spun around and cried out, "Bring them back!"

"I need to find my friends. If you tell me what I need to know, I'll bring them back." I waited for her to decide.

"Bring them back, please!" she pleaded and fell to her knees as tears spilled down her cheeks.

"Help me." I grabbed Claraseve's hands. "Help me and I can get you away from here and back to Earth. You can see these places yourself."

Heavy footsteps filled the corridor outside, and it dawned on me why she kept getting up to fill her drink. She must have pushed a hidden button or summoned them another secret way.

Claraseve pulled her hands away and stood. She wiped the tears off her cheeks and raised her chin. "My life is here, and I play by the rules," she said with a tremble in her voice.

"What have you done? Worlds will perish if I don't find my friends." I searched her face for any ounce of compassion but there was none.

"Then let them perish," she hissed, then louder, "She's in here!"

The door swung open, and a stone creature filled the doorway. Everything about this creature appeared to be solid, from its thighs to its arms and hands. Its stone back rose up behind its stone face with stone eyebrows set above impenetrable eyes, and its lower jaw jutted out and held two stone tusks. The hallway behind him was blocked with more stone men and I knew there was no escape. As the stone man's hand clamped over my arm, Claraseve pounced on my other and darted away with my beloved bracelet in her grasp. I yelled after her and tried to tug my arm free but stone man's grip didn't budge. I winced as my skin tore under its fingers as he shoved me out the door in front of him.

"Move it," a gravelly voice filled my ears. When I didn't move fast enough his hand slammed into my back and sent me sprawling to the floor. Pain seared through my back, and I prayed nothing was broken as I scrambled to my feet and counted guards. There were four of them, one in front, one behind, and one on each side of me. The halls cleared before us as Progos and vasels alike scrambled to get out of their way. The guards didn't talk but moved as one. I had been around military before and recognized the precision and focus. Thoughts of escape flitted through my mind, but I knew I was outnumbered. Besides, security would be on high alert which hampered my ability to find and rescue Miswala and Kokshai. No, for now I just had to see how this played out.

I doubled over in a coughing fit, and expertly took off my necklace and slipped it into my boot, all before stone man could hit me from behind again. I needed information and people talked more freely around those they thought couldn't understand them.

We stopped before a set of heavy double doors. Stone man barked an order and pressed a button on the side of the door.

"What is it?" a voice demanded gruffly through the closed door.

"We have something for Pram," the lead stone guard stated.

"Come back later, we're busy," the voice behind the door demanded.

"Busy getting gored out of your mind, Juxpa? Open up," roared the stone guard.

"One of these days your mouth is going to get you into trouble, Grobler," Juxpa said through the door.

"Any time you want to try my patience I'm ready. I don't answer to anyone but Pram. Now open up," Grobler commanded.

The door opened to reveal large, inky black eyes set in a head crowned by a thick, black, furry mohawk that tapered down its nose and across its cheeks and ran down the length of its sinewy body and tail. Razor sharp teeth gnashed at Grobler who laughed and pushed me through the door into a room that was laid out like a bad mafia movie. Couches and chairs filled the room as half a dozen consorts lounged in skimpy clothes or went without. Glasses littered every surface of the room, all with varying degrees of liquid and other paraphernalia I was not familiar with but could only guess at.

"What am I supposed to do with this?" Juxpa threw his head in disgust in my general direction.

"I really don't care. I wouldn't hurt it too much though. Pram is going to want to find out how it got in here. It doesn't have a crystal," Grobler stated as he eyed my forehead.

"No? Interesting. Yes, he'll want to see it. Can it understand us or talk?" Juxpa asked.

"How in Pram's name would I know that? I don't talk to prisoners," Grobler grumbled.

Juxpa leaned towards me, tilting its head, and said," It's almost time for my feeding. I think after Pram is done with you, I'll take a limb or two to snack on. While you're still awake. Have you ever heard bones popping as the skin rips?"

I replied politely that he could take his snack and put it somewhere, but since I didn't have my translator on it remained gibberish to him.

He turned towards Grobler. "I don't think it understands. Put it in a cage in Pram's room."

Grobler picked me up by my arm but dropped me when the front door of the suite opened. A creature that resembled Juxpa—with the exception of some grey in his black fur—strode in followed by a large, extremely muscular bodyguard with green skin and eyes, and long pointed tusks. I noticed a peculiar look pass between Grobler and the green guard and did my best to seem disinterested in everything.

"Pram, we weren't expecting you back yet." Juxpa's voice rose an octave in fear.

"Obviously." Heavy sarcasm dripped from Pram's words. "Clear out the room, now!"

"Right away Pram." Juxpa uttered an expletive and the consorts scurried across the room and out the door without a backward glance.

"What have we here?" Pram eyed me as I sat in a heap at Grobler's feet.

"Claraseve reported a stranger in her rooms, and we found this," Grobler replied.

"I see. What is it? Does it talk?" I eyed Pram with a vacant stare, alarm bells going off. This one was dangerous.

"Do you sing pretty, birdie? Is that why you sought out Claraseve? Nothing to say? A few hours with me and you'll sing and tell me everything I want to know. Maybe I should interrogate Claraseve too. Hmmmm?"

"She's too scared of losing privileges to risk anything," Grobler stated.

"You may be right, but I'd still like to ask her some questions. After her show, of course. These Progos eat her up. Now where shall I put you as I have some pressing business to attend to? There's some cells in the lower levels. I could make it a show with the Progos."

"I wouldn't."

"Oh? And why is that Grobler?" Pram's eyes narrowed dangerously.

"It doesn't have a crystal so it must have been smuggled in by one of the Progos. Do you want to tip your hand and let them see that you captured it?"

Pram rubbed his chin in silence.

"You may be right, Gobler, and as always, I trust your instincts. These Progos are getting creative. Thargon," Pram gestured towards his large, green bodyguard, "put her in the back room. If anything, it'll make a good addition to my zoo and leave the Progo responsible wondering if I know anything, which gives me the upper hand," Pram purred.

Thargon grabbed me around the waist, threw me under his arm, and carried me to the back room. It was smaller, with a row of three cubes that lined one wall. He opened one, threw me in, closed the door, leaned against the wall, and waited. I huddled in the corner and buried my face in my cloak, trying to look weaker than I was. I have found that by using this method, captors tend to underestimate you and make mistakes. After a few minutes Grobler entered.

"Pram wants to find out what the holdup is."

"Is everything in place?"

"Can we talk in front of it?"

"It can't understand."

Grobler nodded. "I have my men waiting."

"Good. I can't handle dealing with his stupidity much longer. He has the power to rule galaxies and wastes it on those stupid Progos." Thargon spat out.

"Soon the Progos will bow before you. Shreg's close to figuring out how to harness its energy," Grobler murmured.

"Get word to him and the others that we need to accelerate the timeline. Pram wants to waste its energy on giving the Progos more youth." Thargon sneered.

"He never could think past the money. We should get back though so he doesn't get suspicious."

"He would never expect this." Thargon walked over to a cylindrical tube in the far corner of the room and stroked it. "As for you my wondrous creature, you're the answer I've been looking for."

I risked a look and shock rocketed through my body as my eyes locked with Miswala's.

16) Deprama 3

As soon as Thargon and Grobler left the room I focused on the container that imprisoned Miswala. Its smooth sides rose from ceiling to floor, with a small control panel on the front. We couldn't hear each other, and Miswala couldn't pass through the walls, which meant it was designed to somehow hold energy.

I mouthed Kokshai and Miswala looked towards the other corner where Kokshai lay still. I held my breath and counted until I saw Kokshai twitch. It was alive for now. I inspected my prison for any way out. Two of the walls were concrete and the other walls were made of a strong, clear substance with no visible door hinges or handles. I ran my fingers over every inch and was no closer to finding an escape when I heard footsteps coming down the hall. I huddled in the corner of the cage opposite the door and gestured for Miswala to be still. Pram walked in followed closely by a tall creature shrouded in grey with a face that disappeared behind a mist. They stopped in front of Miswala.

"Are you close to figuring out how to siphon its energy, Shreg?" Pram asked.

"Getting there. This one is much different than the other creatures we've used." the shrouded figure responded.

"I don't care! You're the scientist so you need to figure this out now. The other source won't last a week. The only reason the Progos kept me alive is because of that youth serum. If they figure out we're almost out, things will go very bad for all of us. There's already been some rumors, which I've put a stop to before it gets to the wrong Progos." Pram paced in front of Miswala's cage. "All that time, money, resources, and planning wasted! I still can't figure out how the door closed when it did. Osswa must have done something wrong. It should have stayed open long enough for us to collect hundreds of them, not just one!" Pram chewed on a claw as he eyed Miswala. "No, something else happened, something I can't quite figure out."

"At least we have this one," Shreg said.

"Which won't mean much if you don't figure out a way to inject its energy into the serum!" Pram shouted as spittle hit Miswala's container.

Shreg put a hand on the container. "I know my method will work. I just need to run some tests on it first."

Pram gnashed his teeth. "I said no tests. I don't want to waste any of it. No telling how long until we get back there so we need to make this one last."

Shreg dropped his hand and lowered his voice. "You can either let me run some tests in my lab which will speed up the process, or it can remain in here and it could take me weeks. It's up to you, Pram."

Pram stopped pacing to glare in Shreg's direction and pointed a sharp claw at him.

"Fine, you get your wish but if you waste even a single drop—"

"Threats? I thought we were past that."

"You have two days. Two." Pram's voice rose an octave as he stormed out of the room.

"You have no idea how important you are, do you? Mmmmm, the weapons we'll create using your energy. I can't wait to see the destruction and when he finds a way to your planet, which he will, oh, the possibilities! Weapons on such a massive scale it's never been seen. All those sources of beautiful energy. It's so delicious to think of the terror and destruction that will ensue." Shreg shuddered and dropped his hand as Thargon strode into the room.

"Pram sent me to get you whatever you needed." Thargon's twisted smile stretched across his face.

"I've bought some time for you, but it'll have to be moved to my lab tonight."

Not long after Thargon and Shreg left, I heard voices approaching.

"Pram wants to ask me some questions, Juxpa, that's all I know. I'll wait for him in the chamber." A familiar female voice said.

"I'm not sure Pram wants you back there. Maybe you should wait here with me," Juxpa purred.

"I'll wait in the chamber. I've heard too many stories about you," the familiar voice replied.

"You cut me."

"Look, let's call a truce and have a drink while I wait. I have some toku," the female said.

"Well, maybe one," Juxpa said.

I listened as the voices grew louder and quickly put my necklace back on.

"Love what he's done with the place," Claraseve said as she walked into the room and shuddered at the vicious weapons that occupied the wall across from my cell.

"He's skilled at getting answers. Now let's have a taste." Juxpa eagerly eyed the bottle in Claraseve's hands.

"Of the toku," Claraseve said as she took a small flask out of a bag slung across her shoulders.

"Of course. Wouldn't dream of hurting Pram's star singer." Juxpa eyed Claraseve up and down while he unscrewed the cap. He took a large swig and passed it back. Claraseve held my gaze and barely tilted her head towards Juxpa before she mimicked taking a drink and put the flask away. It didn't take long before Juxpa stumbled and slurred his words.

"Is the room spinning? I feel like the room is spinning." Juxpa shook his head and collapsed onto the floor as loud snores escaped his mouth.

"What did you give him?" I asked Claraseve.

"It's a very potent sleeping potion. I had it smuggled in from the market on the outskirts of town. I took a huge risk, but some fans can get very . . . demanding. They never remember anything later except waking up with a monstrous headache." Claraseve smirked and then turned serious. "Can you really get me out of here and back to Earth, or did I just waste my toku on him?" Claraseve held up my bracelet.

"I can, but we have to get my friend out of there." I pointed towards Miswala. "But why are you willing to risk it all now? You said before—"

"I know what I said. That was before I knew my world really existed. That I could have another life besides this one and that made me feel something I've never felt before."

"It's called hope. How do you open the door?"

Claraseve darted over to Juxpa and slipped off an ornate ring with a crystal that seemed to reflect all the colors, and yet none of the colors.

"This is our ticket out and will open any door in the city," Claraseve said.

"We need to get Miswala and Kokshai and get back to the door to their planet. From there I can take you home."

"Where's the door located?" Claraseve asked as she placed the ring by the door. A small click and the door slid open to my freedom.

"It's on the surface, hidden unless you know what to look for," I said and squeezed her arm in gratitude before darting over to Miswala's prison.

"Then we need to hurry. Pram will be back in a few hours, and it will take a while to reach the surface," Claraseve said.

"Even worse, Thargon will be here soon to take Miswala to Shreg's lab," I said with a grim face.

Claraseve passed the ring over the control panel and with a pop, it opened up. Miswala flew past us over to Kokshai.

"Kokshai's not doing well, Merelda, and neither am I. We need to get home." Miswala's voice was weak and wispy.

"Thank you would have been nice," Claraseve replied, arms crossed.

"Thank you. Now can we go home?"

"That's the plan." I scooped up Kokshai, opened my bag and placed it in. "I know it's not the most prestigious way to travel but it'll have to do."

"Now what? I don't know the surface well so I can't help find the door." Claraseve stood stoic and I was humbled by the amount of trust she had in me, considering what she had risked helping us.

"We need to get down to the lower levels. I can retrace my steps and get us back to the door," I said and hoisted my bag and Kokshai to my back, under my cloak.

"There are multitudes of lower levels. You need to be more specific," Claraseve said.

I described the chamber to Claraseve and her face drained of all its color for the second time that day, "You never said anything about going there."

"I have to go back to retrace my steps, Claraseve. There's no other way, I'm sorry. We have to go down there."

She drew a shaky breath and nodded.

"Good, what about him?" I asked and nodded towards Juxpa snoring on the floor.

"The toku should last for a few more hours. We can leave him but before we go out there we need to go over some important rules. Don't speak to anyone. Don't look at anyone. Just walk purposefully and follow me. No one should bother us and Juxpa's ring will get us into places; this," she tapped the crystal on her forehead, "won't. If anyone does stop you, simply say you are on an errand for Pram. You don't know that errand, but you were given instructions. No one wants to get on Pram's bad side so they should leave us alone."

"What about you and your fans?"

"They're only allowed to approach me at a show, or right after. Everyone here knows that. They may say something in passing but that's it."

"Miswala, grab onto my bag and hold on. No one should be able to see you under my cloak and we need to keep you well hidden."

"Ready?" I asked Claraseve, and she knew I meant more than just heading out the door.

She nodded her head and steadied herself.

"Whatever comes, thank you. I could never have lived knowing there was another possibility of another life for me. Hope, you called it. For me it was an awakening. And I never want to go back to sleep."

"Then let's go."

17) Deprama 4

Claraseve strode down the wide corridor, keeping to the sides and out of the way of the Progos as I followed behind, head down and hidden behind my cloak. Music, barely discernible, trailed behind me and was lost in the muffle of the crowd as they strolled to their destination. Miswala's music was weak, which right now was a double-edged sword. It meant it wouldn't be noticeable, but it also meant they were fading. I pushed that thought path down and concentrated on the back of Claraseve's head. We would be back in time. There were no other options.

Claraseve's shoulders drew up as a god-awful alarm blared down the corridor, insistent in its angry repetition to be heard, followed by flashing red lights. Everyone froze and cast uneasy looks up at the alarms. Claraseve looked over her shoulder and locked eyes with me as she struggled to control her panic. We quickened our steps as the sound of heavy feet approached us accompanied by yells of outrage as armed guards pushed aside the Progos who did not get out of their way fast enough. The Progos dropped their act of indignation and scurried back to the safety of their rooms when fighting broke out between groups of guards, adding to the confusion.

Claraseve and I skirted the fight and ran full speed down the hall, all pretense gone. Why were the guards fighting each other? It didn't make any sense. Unless Thargon had seized the opportunity and used the confusion of our escape to launch his uprisings. He was either very smart or very ambitious, which was dangerous either way. It also meant both sides would be looking for us. We turned a corner and skidded to a halt before a group of armed guards coming down the hall towards us. The leader yelled something at us as we backtracked and ran down another passage.

Claraseve veered down a small alcove and used Juxpa's ring to enter another wing. We raced through a room filled with exotic plants. Some hanging, some planted, some behind glass, and still others in various stages of being harvested for either medicinal or recreational use but I guessed was for the latter. Just as we reached the opposite side and opened a door to another room, the guards burst into the plant room. The leader's eyes narrowed. "Claraseve!"

Claraseve didn't slow as we tore through room after room. One room was filled with unbelievably large, spherical, water orbs, suspended in the air, each containing complete ocean systems from different planets.

"Don't touch any! You'll be sucked in and drown!" Claraseve shouted just as a guard's head skimmed the bottom of an orb and was pulled in. The other guards gaped as he was snapped in half by a sea creature whose eyes had followed them eagerly. We didn't stay long enough to see what happened next.

"Stay to the sides!"

"What is it?" I eyed the large sunk-in tubs, each filled with different foul-smelling concoctions that dotted the floor before us.

"You don't want to know." Claraseve grimaced.

A guard shouted and I risked a look back as he fell into a vat which quickly consumed him and turned a putrid green.

"Merelda!" Claraseve screeched and I pulled back just as a tub erupted in front of me. I skirted it carefully and joined Claraseve on the other side as we raced on into the last room in the wing. This one was filled floor to ceiling with glutinous food. Vasels stuffed progos full while they lounged on daises, too engorged to move, indifferent to the commotion as we sped past. We skidded to a stop and backed away as more armed guards entered the room through the door we had been running to.

I knew we were trapped with no way out. I grasped Claraseve's hand and withdrew a small weapon that was of no use against twenty trained armed guards. The guards behind us approached, leers turning into snarls as they recognized the other group of guards. War cries erupted and both groups rushed each other as we dove out of the way behind stunned Progos. Blood soon covered the floor and made it slick as each side inflicted lethal wounds with horrific weapons. One guard raised his knife in the air only to gape as his chest disintegrated and he toppled to the ground in two pieces.

I tugged on Claraseve and we escaped amid the confusion and chaos. No one stopped us as we continued running down corridors filled with smoke.

"Do you know where we are?" I asked as I held my side and gasped for air. My device couldn't keep up with the strenuous demands and I felt my lungs burn.

"Yes, we're nowhere near *those* chambers but we have to keep moving."

"We need to get back to the door!" I argued.

"I realize that but I'm trying to not get us killed!" Claraseve shouted.

"Touche," I murmured and tried to slow my breathing.

We pushed on and only stopped when we got to the end of the city. An enormous bay opened up before us, filled with vendors, and pods for spacecrafts to park while they unloaded their wares.

"What is this place?" I asked.

"It's the black market. If we can get down there we can hide in one of the trucks used to transport Pram's inventory to the main building. From there we should be able to backtrack to the door."

"It looks calm down there."

"The alarms don't reach here. These guys are jumpy enough as it is, and it would clear out if they heard alarms, which is bad for business. Pram will want to keep a lid on this."

"What if Thargon wins?"

"That's an extremely long shot."

"So was finding a human on this planet."

"Touche."

We looked up as shouts were heard from above and below.

"Run!" I shouted to Claraseve.

And we were off again as chaos broke out around us. Fighting factions spilled into the bay, and vendors scrambled to throw their stolen merchandise into crafts and flee the planet. We ducked into the belly of an aircraft as a group of armed guards ran past. We were just about to dash across to the trucks when the door slammed, and the spaceship lurched into the air.

"I don't give a damn what you guys say, Kubal, I'm out of here. I'm not getting involved in planet politics. Shoot me down, then, if you can. Dammit!!! He's really shooting at me!!! HA! My ship can outfly anything you send my way Kubal!! Wooooo!!!" a voice shouted from the cockpit of the ship.

Claraseve and I looked at each other, as the implications set in. I put my finger to my lips and motioned her to stay put. I set my bag and Miswala on the ground gingerly and crept up to the cockpit before a voice stopped me in my tracks, "You may as well come and introduce yourselves since you're on my ship. And don't think about trying to steal this beauty, or I'll drop you at the next planet which isn't much better than Deprama."

I walked towards the voice on wobbly legs still not recovered from running. He swiveled his chair around and I came face-to-face with a dark teal alien with human features.

"Bring the others up. My ship doesn't look like it, but appearances are deceiving. I knew you were here the minute I got on board."

"Then why didn't you kick us off?"

"I was in a bit of a hurry, if you didn't notice the battle happening around us, and I figured if you were smart enough to get this far, who was I to stand in your way to freedom. Now get the others so we can talk and I can figure out what to do with you."

I nodded and went back for the others.

"Don't speak unless he asks you a direct question, and even then, let me answer. We don't know who this guy is or what his intentions are," I told the others.

Claraseve nodded and frowned. "What about the door, Merelda? How are we going to get back to it?"

"It's actually Esmerelda," I replied absently as I tried to formulate a plan. "We may be able to force him to drop us off on the surface, somehow. Or we can give him some of your toku."

"Do you know how to fly a ship?" Claraseve asked in wonder.

"Well, no, I never got around to learning to fly a spaceship like this, but I can fly a basic model, so this one can't be too different."

Claraseve eyed me with doubt, sighed, and got up from her seated position.

"Miswala, stay out of sight under my cloak. We can't risk you being seen until we know what his plans are."

The teal alien met us at the entrance to the cockpit and gestured down the hall.

"We may as well be comfortable as we talk. I don't know about you, but adrenaline always makes me hungry."

With no other choice we proceeded him down the hall. The

immediate danger had passed but there was still the danger Miswala would be discovered and taken back. After all, he had been at the black market and that was usually filled with thieves who were not the most trustworthy. Then of course, there was the little problem of getting Miswala and Kokshai home. I wasn't sure how long they would last away from their planet but by the looks of them, they had days, if that.

"If you guys are thinking of attacking me the ship is programmed to shoot you down if it senses my heart has stopped," he replied nonchalantly, as if reading my mind. He motioned us through a door as it slid open to reveal some sort of kitchen. A table and chairs occupied the center of the room and he motioned for everyone to sit.

"Are you guys hungry?" the teal alien asked. "I may have some Earth food." He grinned as my head shot back in surprise at both the offer of food and knowing where Claraseve was from.

"You're an awfully long way from home. All of you." He looked down at Kokshai, who munched the corner of my cloak where blue sand had gotten stuck in the seams.

I gasped and tried to pick Kokshai up, but it was firmly clamped onto my cloak.

"At least Kokshai's looking a bit better, Merelda." Miswala flowed out from under my cloak. "Don't be angry, Merelda," Miswala begged as my face betrayed my agitation. "He won't betray us."

"And how do you happen to know that?" I demanded.

"I just do."

"I think some introductions are in order."

"I don't think we have time for this," I interrupted. Since he knew about Miswala and Kokshai there was no reason not to ask for passage back to Deprama. "We need to get back to the surface of Deprama."

"In case you didn't notice, there's a war going on. I'm not risking this ship or my life just to get you back to a miserable planet. In fact, you should be thanking me for getting you off there! Now, we are going to continue with introductions so I can get a feel for you THEN I am going to figure out what to do with you. Is that clear?"

"Crystal," I replied icily. It looked like our only chance was to give him the toku. I'd have to ask Claraseve for it and see if I could find an opportunity to administer it. Worse case, we may have to physically restrain him and make him drink it. I eyed his muscles and thought of his defense system. What was the alternative if I didn't try?

The teal alien sat on the counter and looked us over before he continued. "My name's Bethtizmo, and I'm from Aracna."

"Claraseve."

"Earth," Bethtizmo replied as she nodded.

"Miswala."

"Trilesk," Bethtizmo replied as again my head jerked back in surprise.

"Esmerelda," I said, angry at myself for being eager to hear what he had to say. I had known from a young age that I was from another dimension, but unfortunately, over the centuries, the knowledge of our origins had been lost.

"I'm not sure and that is an anomaly. I always know where beings are from just by looking at them." He seemed perplexed.

"Is everyone from your planet like you?" Claraseve asked as she toyed with her bag.

Bethtizmo's eyes clouded over. "There is no one else. I'm the only survivor after my planet was destroyed."

We all looked down in silence as his sorrow filled the room.

"What were you doing on Deprama?" I finally asked and broke the silence.

"Looking for information."

"What kind of information?" I asked with narrowed eyes.

"Nothing that would interest you. I'm after information on my partner. He was taken by raiders. There was a merchant's war going on and they needed soldiers so they came and took everyone that could fight and killed the rest. I was away when it happened and when I came back he was gone. Sol had been taken. I traded or sold all our things and bought this beauty." Bethtizmo smiled at the ship and continued. "Markets like the one on Deprama are a treasure trove of information. Some good, some bad, but there's always something. In exchange for information, I supply the informants with things I've picked up, usually things that can be sold for a quick profit."

"You steal?"

"From thieves, yes I do."

"Is that why Kubal was firing at you?"

"Kubal gave me a bad tip last time, so he owed me a free tip this time. He didn't see it that way. Difference of opinion."

"And he almost shot you down for that?"

"He was grumpy. Enough of me. Why were you on Deprama? You don't have a crystal and you don't seem like a Progo, so what were you doing there?" Bethtizmo jutted his chin towards my forehead.

I quickly filled Bethtizmo in from the time Miswala was taken to when we ducked into his ship, with some omissions about the interest in using Miswala's energy. I still didn't trust him even if Miswala did.

He sat in silence for a few minutes and mulled over the information.

"So, you need to get back to Deprama, to get to the door to return Miswala and Kokshai, otherwise they die and eventually their world and all the others will end."

"That about sums it up," I replied as an alarm went off down the hall.

"What is that?"

"Not sure." Bethtizmo scrambled to the deck. When he pulled up a screen, an image of Thargon holding Pram's head jolted the group.

"I guess it wasn't such a long shot," murmured Claraseve.

"I am Thargon, Ruler of Deprama. For all you Progos, Deprama is permanently closed. You no longer have access to your infantile youth serum. This is no longer your playground. Do not waste your time trying to get your pitiful serum as it has been destroyed. Do not attempt to invade Deprama's atmosphere or land here as you will be destroyed. Any attempt against me or Deprama, you will be destroyed. Those that are still on Deprama and wish to leave will pay an exit fee, payable now, or face death. Those that want to stay and join my army—"

Grobler appeared on the screen, whispered in Thargon's ear, and departed.

"It appears that some of you doubt me. You will learn."

The screen went dark and moments later a massive destroyer appeared.

"Someone is not messing around. That weaponry is no joke," Bethtizmo murmured.

"I thought we were out of their atmosphere," Claraseve's voice trembled.

"We are. This guy is broadcasting it throughout the galaxy. Apparently, he wants to send a message."

A large beam of light shot from the surface of the planet hit the ship and in a split second, it disintegrated completely. The others stared at the screen in horror as Thargon came back on the screen.

"Do not doubt my weaponry or ability to use them again. I will destroy you. This is your last warning."

Bethtizmo turned to the others, "Let's hope your Earth saying is true."

"What saying?"

"When one door shuts another opens, because that door has effectively been slammed shut."

18) Kate's Mom

The last trace of the vision dissipated as Kate gradually came to, and she took in a deep, shuddering breath. Goosebumps rose on her arms as she peeled her sweat soaked shirt from her skin, and cool air rushed in. It seemed the further she read and experienced, the more of a toll it took on her. Exhausted, she stayed slumped in the chair until slowly she became aware of whispering. Faint, but insistent it gnawed at her, demanding to be noticed. She listened, head cocked and tried to pinpoint its location. There. It seemed to be coming from behind the bookcase.

With a groan she got up and examined the shelves crammed with books and knick knacks. The back panel appeared solid, but in the house that didn't mean much. She drew back and let her eyes drift over the volumes until she noticed a pattern of symbols on the spines that she recognized. Aunt Esme had used the same symbols when she signed Kate's Christmas and birthday cards. At the time Kate thought it was a weird quirk, but now she was grateful for her aunt's persistence.

With trembling hands she pulled the books out towards her. They stopped halfway, stuck, but nothing else happened. She pushed the books back into the bookcase and tried a reverse order with no results. Maybe she had missed a symbol. Arms crossed, she tapped her finger on her arm and studied them. Seven symbols, some with wiggling lines, others with swirls and dots; each one different. They were the same color as the books, and she suspected it was to make them blend in. No, she hadn't missed one. She had pulled them in the correct order as her aunt had written them. Maybe it wasn't supposed to be that order. Maybe Kate was supposed to figure this out on her own. Lost in concentration, she didn't notice the whispering had picked up until the symbols began to burn, brighter and brighter, and something small broke loose in Kate.

Shocked, she looked and realized the symbols were actually letters and she knew what it spelled, even if she didn't know what it meant. Quickly she pulled the books down in the correct order, *H A R R I K A N*. A moment later the bookcase swung out to reveal a small piece of metal, the size of a plaque, embedded in the wall. Its smooth surface was marred only by a single thumbprint directly in the center. Kate placed her thumb on top of the print, and a second later cried out and stuck her thumb in her mouth. A drop of her blood raced through the grooves and she watched mesmerized. When it reached the end, the door swung open to reveal a small, orange, silk bag.

She reached in and pulled out the bundle of tied fabric. Her fingers worked the knots until they gave way and revealed a brilliant orange crystal, unlike anything she had ever seen. Tear-shaped and smooth, with a fire that glinted deep within. A seamless, worn, leather strap wound its way through a hole in the top, and she slipped it over her head without another thought. The crystal lurched as it landed over her heart and she was eight again with Aunt Esme.

"It's been in our family for a very long time," her aunt said as she removed the necklace from the safe. "Rumors have been handed down through the generations that it's a special key and one day a Harrikan will take it up and know how to use it. Until then we keep it safely locked away. Each new traveler must promise to help protect it. Will you do that Kate? Help protect it and keep it hidden?"

"It doesn't want to be hidden anymore," Little Kate said as she stared intently at the crystal that burned in the center.

"How do you know what it wants?" And Aunt Esme looked at eight-year-old Kate strangely.

The memory faded into a vision of her aunt, in chains, weak and filthy huddled on the floor somewhere. She looked up, and Kate's head jerked back at the gauntness. Her aunt's eyes widened as they focused on Kate and the necklace.

"The key must be protected! Don't let him get it!"

And then blackness and screaming. Kate came to, on the floor and gasped for air. Her legs trembled as she stood and slowly made her way to the others. She needed to tell them what she just saw.

The audible sound of voices carried down the hall, and Kate followed them to the kitchen. Mrs. B and Maggie looked up, and their smiles froze when they saw Kate's ashen face. They both jumped up and guided her to a chair.

"What happened?" Mrs. B asked, eyebrows furrowed.

"I'm really not sure," Kate said and launched into details of what had just transpired, omitting the part about the whispering. She didn't want them to think she was hearing voices. No, that wasn't quite right. She didn't *want* to share that part. Something about the crystal spoke to her and she didn't want the others to know just yet.

Mrs. B's eyebrows furrowed deeper. "Did you see anything in the vision that could help us know where she's being held?"

"No, I didn't." Kate's shoulders slumped as a wave of exhaustion washed over her. The vision confirmed that her aunt was being held somewhere and it shook Kate. It was one thing to suspect, another to know.

Mrs. B pressed Kate. "Do you think the necklace is a key?"

"I don't know. Maybe? If it is, I have no idea what it opens."

Maggie eyed first the crystal and then Kate. "What if it's dangerous?"

Kate shook her head. "It's not and before you ask me how I know. I just do."

Mrs. B studied the crystal and then Kate for a moment before she spoke. "Maybe it should stay locked away for now. Until we can figure out what it is or what it can do. It might be safer and if your aunt did say to protect it, wouldn't the safe be a better place for it instead of around your neck? And we can't be sure the crystal isn't dangerous either, Kate."

Kate stood up abruptly, toppling the chair back with a crash. Panic filled her at the thought of taking the crystal off and putting it back, but she wasn't sure why. "I know you two are just looking out for me, but you have to trust me on this. I won't put it back in the safe, I won't take it off, and I won't hear any more about it!"

"But if it's dangerous"— Maggie started.

"It's not. I don't know how, but I think it could be useful and honestly, we need all the help we can get right now." Kate replied with an edge to her voice. "Now if you'll excuse me, I need some sleep. I'm exhausted."

"Kate—" Mrs. B called out as Kate rose from the table.

"Whatever it is, it'll have to wait until the morning," Kate replied. She made her way to her room and fell fully clothed onto the bed as sleep welcomed her instantly.

The next morning she woke, still feeling groggy and ventured down the steps into the solarium. The nook still called to her and her fingers itched to pick up a brush, but to what end? Kate's heart sank remembering her conversation with Morgan when she declined the invitation. It was the right thing to do. After all she wouldn't have the time to devote to the show with everything happening at the house. No, it was the right choice, even if it made her sad and, if she was honest, a bit mad, which made her feel guilty.

A small figure carrying a hard case and a tripod, passed by the back and interrupted Kate's train of thought as she did a double take and darted outside after it.

"Hey! Hello?! Yes, you! Who are you and what are you doing here? You know you're trespassing right?" Kate's stern voice hailed a startled young woman in cargo pants.

"Oh! I'm sorry. I was told this property would be vacant."

"You were told wrong, and you still haven't said what you were doing here." Kate crossed her arms and widened her stance.

The woman looked at Kate with a wary gaze. "I was hired to do a land survey before the sale of the house."

"What? The house hasn't sold! When is this supposed sale supposed to take place?" Kate demanded.

"Look, I'm just the surveyor. You'd have to ask whoever is selling the house."

"I plan on it but you need to leave, for your own good." Kate hated how she sounded but it was for the poor woman's safety. Imagine surveying a land and accidentally stepping through a door. I mean, she didn't think that could happen but her education on doors was sorely lacking, and she thought it better to be safe than have someone disappear from her property. That would complicate things needlessly more than they already were.

The woman eyed her warily before she turned and left with a nod. Kate went back inside and almost collided with Maggie, who held a cup of steaming coffee.

"I figured you'd need something stronger than tea. You looked dreadful last night. What was that all about?" Maggie peered over Kate's shoulder where the woman had vacated.

Kate took the coffee with a grateful smile. "Apparently things are moving faster than I expected. That was a surveyor for the property."

"Oh no. What are you going to do?"

Kate took a sip and winced as the hot liquid burned the roof of her mouth.

"I'm going to pay my mom a visit. I need to convince her not to go through with this."

"What if she doesn't listen? She's not known for that, you know." Maggie looked at Kate with compassion. She knew more than anyone else how complicated her relationship with her mother was.

Kate gulped down some more coffee. "I don't have a choice. I have to make her listen."

"Are you sure this is a good idea? You still look awful, sorry, and you know you'll need to be on your A game with your mom. I could go with you for emotional support."

Kate grimaced. "I appreciate the offer but this is between me and my mom and I need to do it alone."

"Then you'd better finish that and come to the kitchen for a second cup. You're going to need it."

An hour later Kate walked into the law office where her mother worked. She'd been there a few times in the past and recognized the harried secretary on the phone.

"Is she in?" Kate mouthed. The secretary nodded and waved her through. Kate followed a long hall dotted with doors, each one replete with names in gold lettering, until she stopped at one that read *Janice Jones, Esq.* She took a moment to hide the crystal under her shirt. It had been quiet all morning and Kate hoped it continued. This would be hard enough without distractions. Lifting her chin, she pulled back her shoulders and knocked on the door.

"Come in," her mom's voice rang out. "Kate, what a pleasant surprise. I thought you must have been dead, or kidnapped, or dealing drugs since you never respond to my calls or texts anymore. Please, sit." Her mom gestured to the chair across from her expansive desk. Kate ignored the chair and walked over to the expanse of windows that showed off the view of the city. She knew if she sat down the power would shift and her mom would have the upper hand.

Her mom swung her chair to contemplate Kate. "Well this must be serious. Otherwise you would have texted me or gone to the house. Which means you're either in trouble or need something. So? Which is it?"

Kate took a breath to steady her nerves and plunged on. "You're right. I do want something from you, but it's not what you think. I've been staying at Aunt Esme's house." Her mom drew in a sharp breath, but Kate pushed on. "At first it was just to use the space to paint until the house sold, but some things have happened and now…now I think Aunt Esme's alive."

"I see," her mom said in an icy tone.

Kate risked a glance at her mom's narrowed eyes and thin lips. This had gone so much easier in her mind as she played out the scenario over and over again on the ride over. She rushed on. "I'm sorry I lied to you, but I didn't think you'd understand. Now that you know she might be alive, you can stop the sale of the house."

"So this is what you've been keeping from me. Lying to me, sneaking around behind my back, staying in *that* house. Do you realize you could be accused of breaking and entering? You had no right to be there Kate!" Her mom's voice rose before she stopped to regain her composure. "I'm only going to tell you this one time. You are not to step foot in that house ever again. Do you understand me? I forbid it."

Kate finally turned to face her mother and drew herself up. "You can't go through with this. If you sell the house while she's still alive—"

"She's not. Didn't you know my sister was not mentally stable? There's no telling what happened to her. I *am* moving forward with my plans, and in a few weeks that house will be razed for condos, which will give me great pleasure, I assure you. There are things you don't know about and wouldn't understand."

"No? Like what? What wouldn't I understand?" Kate demanded.

"Don't take that tone with me, young lady. I don't have to explain myself to you. What's done is done."

"I looked up the law. It says she has to be missing for five years to be declared dead and she's only been missing for one." Kate clenched her hands to stop them from shaking.

"Did you honestly just cite the law to me?" her mom asked, incredulous, then laughed. "You may think you know the law, but I know it better. I'm going to prove she was a danger to herself, which means I can bypass the wait period. You don't think I went into this without thinking of all the contingencies and finding all the loopholes, did you? What kind of lawyer would I be if I didn't?"

Kate's heart sank. This was not going as planned. "I won't let you. I'll fight you for it, take you to court."

"By the time you find a lawyer to help you file, it'll be over and the property will be filled with condos. Of course, if it's money you're after, I can give you half of the sale. That should set you up nicely."

"Please mom, you can't do this!" Kate cried.

Her mom stood up and walked over to Kate. With heels she towered over Kate and made her feel like a child.

"I don't want to hear another word about that house! You will NOT step foot into it again or you will force my hand. Do you understand?" Her mom's face darkened with anger and Kate stepped back and with that step, knew she had failed. She thought she was ready for this, strong enough, but she wasn't. Her mom had won again. Shame filled every fiber of her being. She had failed.

Her mom's face flushed with victory. "Now, I have a lot of meetings to prepare for, so you'll have to show yourself out. I appreciate you stopping by, Kate, and I'm glad we could clear the air and come to an understanding. My secretary will see you out."

As if on cue the door opened and the secretary appeared at Kate's elbow. She glanced back at her mom who was typing on her computer as the secretary expertly guided her out of the office.

The car stopped and Kate sagged behind the wheel. How could she face them? Her face flushed and she cringed as her mind replayed the scene over and over again and mocked her. Anger bubbled up but Kate shoved it down. She would find a way to tell them but not yet. She couldn't live through a re-telling right now.

At that moment, Mrs. B and Maggie came down the walk towards the car. Kate stepped out and shook her head and murmured, "Don't ask."

"Well Mrs. B had a great idea if you want to give it a try. Might take your mind off of whatever happened." Maggie said as she rubbed Kate's arm.

Kate managed a half smile and turned towards Mrs. B.

"We know you have the *potential* to see doors, and no one is sure you've never traveled through one right? What if I showed you a door I know is there? A safe one? Try to jog something loose so you can see it?" Mrs. B asked gently.

Kate eyed Mrs. B and tilted her head. "How do you know where a door is? I thought only travelers could see them?"

Mrs, B replied with a smile. "The only door I can see is the door I traveled through to be with your family."

Kate gaped at Mrs. B.

"What? You didn't think I was from around here did you dear? No, I came over after your grandma helped my family. It was my way of trying to pay her back."

"What did my grandma do? Can you go back home? Would you want to?" The thought of Mrs. B leaving brought a lump to Kate's throat.

Mrs. B shook her head and smiled. "Those are stories for another day. Right now let's focus on getting you to see a door."

Kate nodded, still reeling from Mrs. B's revelation. It made sense, but Kate had never thought of it. There was so much she didn't know. They walked in silence for a while until they came upon a circle of rocks covered in moss. Mrs. B gestured towards the middle and Kate stepped through. She walked the perimeter and strained to see the glimmer she knew should be there.

"I can't see anything," Kate said. Her eyes blurred with the effort and frustration crept up.

"Try to let your mind go." Mrs. B suggested.

Maggie shook her head. "No, she needs to try to focus. Or maybe you need to do the thing like with those hidden pictures where you let your eyes unfocus and you can see a picture? Of course, that never worked for me; I could never see them." Maggie harrumphed.

Kate tried again and again but it was no use. She couldn't see the door.

"Try seeing it from outside the circle. Maybe you're too close." Maggie offered.

"We can always try tomorrow. You seem a bit off today, and I know you must still be exhausted." Mrs. B took a step closer to but Kate stopped her with a raised hand.

"It doesn't matter what you say. I can't see anything. No matter how hard I stare, I don't see it!" The last word came out as more of a shout that stopped them in their tracks.

Maggie looked at Kate with concern. "We're just trying to help you figure things out."

Kate knew they were just trying to be helpful, but it became too much. Dark emotions crashed over her as her mind spun out of control. Her aunt was smart, brave, resourceful, and had traveled through who knows how many dimensions helping who knew how many people. Her aunt deserved better than her. Kate could barely do her laundry each week. How could *she* hope to live up to those standards or expectations? What could she do? Hot tears threatened to spill over as Kate's chest tightened in a vice grip. She clenched her fists, slammed them into her thighs, and screamed in frustration.

She felt Maggie and Mrs. B grab her arms, but she yanked away and fell on her knees. Rain started to drizzle and mixed with Kate's tears.

"I can't do it! I can't be like Aunt Esme! I'm not strong enough! I failed at standing up to my mom! I failed at remembering what I needed to! I failed at seeing doors, which means I failed at finding Aunt Esme! I won't be able to stop my mom, and the house will be razed! I'm not a traveler, and everything is falling apart! I can't save her, and I can't save the house. I don't know what I'm supposed to do or remember, and you two aren't helping as much as you think you are. Just leave me alone! You two have no idea what this is like, and you can't help me! No Mrs. B, cookies and tea can't fix this!" Kate shook off Mrs. B's attempts to help her up from the mud.

Mrs. B backed up, touched Maggie's elbow, and turned to go, but Maggie faced Kate, eyes blazing.

"You are being a selfish twatwaffle! That woman is pure gold, and you're going to dump on her like that? When all we've been trying to do is help you, even though we don't understand everything? We've supported you, listened to you, talked with you, and this is how you treat us? Yelling at us and telling us to leave you alone like a child? You need to think about your priorities Kate. I love you but pushing us away is a coward's move and we might not be there when you decide you need us again."

They turned and walked away as Kate collapsed in the mud. She sobbed for what seemed like hours and railed against the unfairness of her situation. They didn't know what it was like. They didn't have the pressure of trying to remember something from twelve years ago that could possibly save her aunt. She just wanted her old life back where the only decision she had to make was what course to take for college or what ramen to eat for dinner. Her mundane life where magic didn't exist. The air whooshed out of her lungs. No. That wasn't right. This was taken away from her once, did she really want to live a life without it again? No. If Kate was completely honest with herself, she loved the thrill of this new life. Yes, she desperately wanted to help save Aunt Esme, but she also wanted a life of adventure like in her aunt's journal. Being able to go through doors and explore other worlds felt right and natural and what she should be doing. She *would* find a way to stop her mom, somehow, and she would practice trying to see the door every day if she had to. She wouldn't give up. Darkness gave way to elation and that's when she saw it. A faint glimmer that hovered in the air. It only lasted for a few heartbeats and then dissolved, but it had been there! Laughter erupted from Kate and she felt a glimmer of hope. There was a chance she could do this, but not alone. She needed her friends.

19) Getting Home 1

Wet footprints trailed Kate up the stairs as she ducked into her room and peeled off her clothes. She toweled off and pulled on leggings and a t-shirt. The self-reflection she had done in the rain had been therapeutic, but now she needed to make some serious amends. It wasn't fair she had taken everything out on her best friends and just hoped they would forgive her.

She found them in the parlor drinking tea as they played a game in comfortable camaraderie. A pang hit her. When had they grown so close? They both ignored her as she approached the table and stopped.

"I'm sorry. I know that doesn't seem adequate but I truly am. I've been so wrapped up in how this affected me; I never thought about how this affected you or how you were doing, which was selfish. I took out my anger and frustration and insecurities on both of you instead of facing them and working through them like an adult." Kate shifted from one foot to the other. "I know this can't have been easy for you guys either, but you've been nothing but supportive and helpful. What can I do to make up for it?"

Maggie and Mrs. B exchanged looks.

"We could make her keep her going. Groveling is an acceptable punishment in my book." Maggie said to Mrs. B.

"She looks like a drowned rat. A very contrite, drowned rat. We should take pity on her." Mrs. B replied.

"I'm not sure. Do you think she's learned her lesson?"

"I have! Please guys. I really am sorry and if it makes you feel better, it tears me up having you mad at me." Kate replied and bit her bottom lower lip to keep it from quivering.

"Ok, I think you've suffered enough. But don't do that again. I hate being mad at you." Maggie said with a straight face before she got up and embraced Kate, followed by a smiling Mrs. B.

"Now what?" Mrs. B asked.

"Well…I can see doors—" Kate began to say.

"Why didn't you tell us?" Maggie interrupted with a grin.

"You were too busy making me grovel, remember?" Kate quipped back with an answering grin. "Anyway, it only lasted a few seconds. I think I can get better with practice but can't go back out there." Kate nodded out the window towards the lightning that filled the sky as the sky broke open and a torrential rainstorm let loose. For now I want to finish reading the journal. Maybe Aunt Esme mentions the crystal, which we still need more info on, or how to make doors stay open longer. It's worth a shot and there's not that much left to read."

"What can we do?" Mrs. B asked from the table.

"Keep watch in case my mother decides to call in the national guard. She won't expect me to disobey but just in case."

"We won't let anyone in," Maggie and Mrs. B replied in unison.

Relieved, Kate went to finish the journal.

Kate took a deep breath and felt the now familiar vertigo as her consciousness tumbled into the journal and her aunt's voice started to talk.

"We have to go back," I said and stared at the screen horrified.

"Did you not just see what they did to that ship? Disintegrated it.

There was nothing left, not a single shred of metal. As in, they are all dead, and no pieces left to put back together dead." Bethtizmo shook his head in disbelief.

"I saw, but we still need to go back somehow. We need to get to that door," I cried, eyes still on the screen.

"What makes you think this ship has better defense equipment than the destroyer?" Bethtizmo asked.

"I don't, but we need to try."

"There is no way we are going back, Esmerelda," Bethtizmo stated matter-of-factly and gestured towards the screen as if that should be proof enough to dissuade me.

"How did Thargon even get a weapon like that?" Claraseve asked as she dropped into a seat. "I mean, if Pram had it, he would have used it on Thargon immediately and none of this would have happened."

"I overheard Thargon talking about using—" I stopped and glanced over at Miswala. I wanted to spare them the harsh truth.

"It's OK, Merelda. I know. Even if I couldn't hear the words, I knew."

I nodded and continued. "Thargon had someone working on a device to extract Miswala's energy to make weapons behind Pram's back. That's what they were working on when we decided it was time to leave."

"Could they have found another energy source?" Bethtizmo asked, eyes still glued to the screen, and shuddered at the thought. "If they had more weapons like that, they would be unstoppable."

"They don't have anything like Miswala or anything from their planet. I would have known."

Claravese spoke up from her chair. "No, not like them, but maybe something else. There were always rumors of ancient beings, held and used for dark things, but they were always whispers. No one dared talk about them, and no one ever saw one, if they even existed."

"From my knowledge of Deprama there were ancient beings that lived on Deprama, but they were all killed once Pram took over." Bethtizmo dropped into the captain's chair and sighed.

"Pram said something back in the chamber I didn't understand at first. He said the last one wouldn't last the week which is why he was so desperate to extract Miswala's energy for the youth serum. He was afraid the Progos would find out and kill him. Maybe he had the last of the ancient beings. Thargon was Pram's personal guard and went everywhere with him. He would know about the ancients. Maybe he used the last of the ancients' energy for a weapon since it wouldn't be used for youth serum," I pondered out loud before I continued. "Thargon's going to have his hands full, but it won't be too long until he figures out we got off the planet before he sends someone after us. I don't think his plan was to stop after taking over Deprama, and he needs Miswala's energy to make weapons. We need to get both Miswala and Kokshai home and close the door that's still open on the surface." I didn't voice my fear that it was already too late and Thargon had found the door, found Aslame and the Trilesks, and that's how he powered his weapon. I didn't want to worry Miswala. They were weak as it was and needed their strength for the journey home.

"How do you propose we do that, Esmerelda?" Bethtizmo looked at me and I shook my head.

"I'm not sure." I paused as something occurred to me. "You knew Claraseve was from Earth, yet Earth isn't in this dimension. Does this mean you're aware of different dimensions?"

"You could say that, yes," Bethtizmo agreed.

"Which means you've met others from different dimensions in your extensive search for Sol, correct? Since you knew where they were from." I went on.

"Again, yes, that is correct."

"Would you have happened to have met a Peradite or know where one is?"

"Why, yes, I happen to know a very eccentric one in the Gromulara Galaxy. She doesn't like visitors, if that's what you're thinking," Bethtizmo said with a shrug.

"I don't care what she likes or doesn't like. The Peradites are brilliant, talented inventors and tinkerers, and the only ones who even might be able to create what we need."

"Which is?" Claraseve asked. She looked at home in the copilot's chair. I brushed the thought away and continued.

"A device to open and close doors of course," I replied.

"Of course." Claraseve's voice dripped sarcasm. "Just that easy? They can just whip something up for us to get Miswala and Kokshai home?"

"You've never known a Peradite, seen one at work, or used any of the technology they've created. I have. Over my years of traveling, I've used countless devices invented by them. I'm confident they are the only ones that can figure something out to help us," I replied with more confidence than I felt. So many things could go wrong, but I refused to dwell on them. I had been in worse situations, although not many topped this if I was being honest with myself, and everything always worked out. This one would too.

"It's going to take about a day's travel to get to her rock," Bethtizmo said with a grin.

"Rock?"

"I told you she was a bit eccentric. She lives on a small, barren asteroid. Of course, she may not even let us land once she knows it's me." Bethtizmo's smile turned wry.

"If she agrees?" I asked with a frown.

"Last time she may have chased me off after I did an emergency landing on her rock. I needed a place to hide from grifters that were after me."

"Grifters?" Claraseve asked, confused. "What are those?"

"Soulless, horrid, sadistic beings." Bethtizmo shuddered. "It's better to pray for death than let them catch you. What they don't eat or enslave, they sell to—well, trust me, you'd rather be dead than any of those options. So, I hid on her rock, and she didn't like it much. I would like to think she was warming up to me at the end."

"I thought you said she chased you off."

"Actually, it was more of a mutual decision. She threatened to blow up my ship, and I felt the need to leave." Bethtizmo looked at his fingernails with sudden interest and avoided looking at me.

"Why would she threaten to blow up your ship?" I stepped in front of him and forced him to look at me and held his gaze. He squirmed in his chair and then spoke.

"Look, originally when I landed, I begged her to let me stay a week. She reluctantly agreed with the condition that I stay on my ship. Where we started to disagree was my invasion of her solitude after the first week. I saw it as being safe. She saw it as invading her sanctity. I had just stocked up on supplies so had plenty to last. I offered her some as payment, sort of rent for the space, and she laughed at me. Called it space garbage and told me to stuff it. After that we bickered every day. After a few weeks she threatened to blow up my ship with me in it if I didn't leave, so I thought it was time for me to go."

"Why did you stay that long?"

Bethtizmo shuddered. "You have obviously never had a run-in with grifters. If so, you wouldn't be mocking me, Esmerelda."

"I'm not mocking you. I'm just trying to understand what we're going into." I quickly went through different scenarios and how best to deal with them so I would be prepared when I met the Peradite.

"Well, don't say I didn't warn you. I'll set the coordinates, and you can figure out what to say to get her to agree to let us land. You guys should get some rest while you can. There are beds down the hall on the left."

"I'll help if that's OK," Claraseve offered to Bethtizmo. "I can't sleep, and I'd like to watch the stars. We didn't see them on Deprama."

Bethtizmo nodded. I gathered Kokshai up in my arms and walked down the hall to the beds. Once there I turned towards Miswala who had followed. "How are you holding up? I haven't had a chance to ask you in all of this."

"We'll be better once we're home. I fear Kokshai is fading. Although the sands they found on your cloak helped, they need to eat enormous amounts the first week. I can hear Kokshai, but it's fading and it scares me, Merelda."

"We'll get you home soon. Until then, try to rest."

Miswala looked off. "Can I tell you something, Merelda?"

"Anything."

"I thought my life was boring before. I used to explore just to break up the monotony and imagine what life looked like on other planets. And then I met you, and you were wonderful, and I loved you and you told stories and made life interesting. And then I was chosen when I never thought I would be, and I had purpose and was connected to Kokshai. When they came and took me, Kokshai wouldn't let go of me, so they had no choice but to take it. I thought it was a mistake that Kokshai chose me, that I had caused all of this. But now I think M'ra knew all along. How did you come to Trilesk that day?"

"I literally fell through. I put my hand on the painting to steady myself while putting my boots on and the rest you know."

"Do you think M'ra did all this knowing we would need you to save us? Save the worlds?"

"I think if M'ra had me as a backup plan in case this happened, I'm OK with it."

I stretched and stifled a yawn as I sat down on the bed. Exhaustion pulled at me and made it hard to think. "I need to get some sleep for just a few hours, Miswala. I have to be ready for whatever lies ahead."

"Good night, Merelda. And thank you for coming for us."

I nodded and fell back onto the bed and sweet oblivion.

20) Getting Home 2

I heard muffled shouting and slowly started to make out words as my mind surfaced from a deep sleep.

"Esmeralda, you need to get up!" Claraseve shouted as she shook me.

In an instant I was awake and on my feet.

"Is it Thargon?"

"It's grifters!" Claraseve grimaced. "We need to get to the flight deck; the others are already there."

The ship turned sharply and threw us against the wall.

"Sorry!" Bethtizmo's voice came over the intercom. "But I suggest you guys hurry."

We did as asked and hurried to the flight deck and found our seats just as the ship lurched again.

"Hang on!" Bethtizmo yelled as I buckled into my seat and Claraseve slipped into the chair next to him.

He pushed a lever all the way down and the ship accelerated forward as the force pressed us into our seats.

"Can we outrun them?" I yelled.

Bethtizmo and Claraseve both ignored me as they worked the controls. I watched, amazed as Claraseve took cues and direction from Bethtizmo. She looked like she had been doing this her whole life.

Bethtizmo must have shown her how to work the controls while I slept, but she obviously had some aptitude for it to be so quick so soon.

I held on, thankful for the full harness belt that kept me in place as the ship rolled and tumbled. My stomach lurched as the ship dove straight down at an asteroid.

"What are you doing?"

"Trust me, Esmerelda! They always go left."

"Are you sure you know what you're doing?"

"Can we really be sure of anything? And I REALLY need to concentrate!" he yelled before the ship veered off at the last second to the right, while the grifters veered to the left.

"Ha! I told you they always go left," Bethtizmo shouted as he continued to work the controls.

"Don't celebrate too soon. They're still back there." Claravese pointed to the screen where the grifters' ship could be seen coming up behind them again.

"I see that," Bethtizmo said from between clenched teeth. "We can't outrun them. We need—"

"What is that?" I spied something off to the left. A shimmer. Could that be? A door out here? That seemed unlikely but still . . . "There, to the left! Do you see that?"

"That's a wormhole and before you ask, no, we can't go through it. We don't have the energy force needed to get through safely. We'll have to find another way to outrun the grifters."

"Go through it," Miswala said as they floated from their seat.

"You can't be serious! We could be torn apart in there!"

"We won't, Bethtizmo. Trust me," Miswala replied with a serene smile. Their eyes closed and their body began to glow brighter and brighter as the spaceship hurled towards the spherical entrance to the wormhole.

"Hang on, everyone!" he yelled, and the ship plunged into the swirling blackness that yawned deep just as Miswala's brilliance expanded to fill every crevice of the ship, blinding everyone until they emerged on the other side.

Shocked silence ensued, broken only by heavy breathing. I unbuckled my harness and slid to the floor next to Miswala, who was now normal size.

"Are you OK?"

"Yes, I'm OK, just drained. I'll be OK in a bit, I promise, Merelda."

"Well, that was something." Claraseve eyed Miswala. "How did you do that?"

"I'm not sure. I just knew what to do."

"But how—"

"Enough. Miswala's exhausted and needs to rest," I said, mouth set in a firm line. I ushered my friend down the hall and into a quiet room with Kokshai.

"Rest here. I'll come get you if there are any developments." I closed the door and headed back to the flight deck.

"How bad did the wormhole throw us off course?" I asked Bethtizmo who smiled wide.

"It actually pushed us closer. We should be there within a couple of hours if you want to get some more rest."

I shook my head. "I'm OK. I'm wide-awake now, but thanks."

Bethtizmo turned back to the controls. "Did you know they could?" he asked and gestured around with one hand.

"No, I didn't." I sighed. "And I don't want to speculate on how they did it or what more they're capable of, for their safety."

Bethtizmo took the hint and turned his attention back to the controls.

"We're coming up on Nim's place." Bethtizmo pointed to a small asteroid as it came into view.

"Should we announce ourselves?" Claraseve asked.

"She already knows we're here."

An old woman's face filled the screen in the flight deck.

"Bethtizmo, get your ass out of here. I don't like visitors and you overstayed your welcome last time!"

"Nim, it's good to see you! Listen, we've run into a bit of trouble,"

"Don't tell me, grifters. Let them take you this time! I don't run a space hotel and you're not welcome here!"

"But Nim, I have friends that need help—"

"Friends of yours are no friends of mine. Not after you stole my accelerator."

"You stole from her?" I asked incredulously.

"Borrowed. I borrowed it. Added insurance to make sure I got away from the grifters."

"Unless you're bringing back what you 'borrowed,' you have no business here. Now get going before I shoot you down."

I stood up and faced the screen.

"Scaratino," I said, the Peradite dialect feeling alien on my tongue. I was a bit rusty but knew she would understand.

The old woman stopped.

"What did you say?" she asked, eyes narrowed.

"Scaratino," I repeated without breaking eye contact.

The old woman's face hardened as she glared at me. "Park that rust bucket next to the main building. There is a port you can hook up to that will open up into a tunnel. Follow that tunnel into the main building. I'll meet you there." Then the screen went black.

"What did you say?" Bethtizmo asked, stunned by the woman's one-eighty.

"It's a Peradite code. She has to give us sanctuary. Doesn't mean she has to help us, but she has to let us stay."

"Well, that's a useful bit of information," he murmured.

"Don't even think of using it on her again. It's a one-time use only."

Bethtizmo docked the ship, and we walked down the stark white tunnel. We stopped and stared as the tunnel opened up into a large room filled with plants laden with fruits and vegetables of every size that filled every nook of the main building, hung from every surface of the ceiling, and covered every tier of space. Bethtizmo was reaching for a fruit when a sharp voice called out, "Unless you want to die a hideous death I suggest you don't touch that."

"Is that really poisonous?" Bethtizmo asked incredulously.

"Touch it and find out, Bethtizmo. I'll take the joy of watching you writhing around in your own feces payment for my accelerator," the old woman cackled.

He snatched his hand away, placed both behind his back, and backed away from the innocent-looking fruit.

Her smile turned to a scowl as she looked me over head to toe.

"So how does an Eronian know a sacred Peradite word?"

"Eronian! Yes, that makes so much sense now. I'm not sure how I missed that." Bethtizmo's eyes widened in recognition.

"Because you're stupid, Bethtizmo." The old woman glared at Bethtizmo.

"I'm not stupid."

"You are, for joining up with this group. I have a very bad feeling about you lot and my feelings are never wrong."

"How do you know I'm Eronian?" I questioned. I had never heard of Eronia before but felt the rightness of the word on my tongue. Warmth spread and enveloped me from my heart to my fingertips and toes. I finally knew what I was, even if I didn't know anything about my people or my planet. It was a start.

"Because I can see with my eyes, that's how. Now, why are you here? I need to get back to tending my babies," she crooned over a vine spilling off a shelf above her head.

"We need your help with something only you can make. A way to open and close a portal door." I resisted the urge to bombard her with questions about my origins.

"Do you know how difficult that is? How much energy that takes?" The old woman eyed me with disdain.

"I wouldn't ask if we weren't desperate. Please."

"Everyone always is. One of the reasons I left Peradite. People like you, coming in and demanding we make this or that for them. No appreciation. Yet when I needed something, everyone turned on me, all my so-called friends and colleagues. So I left and came here where no one could ask anything of me again. Until you lot showed up."

"What did you need?" I asked, curious as to what would drive a Peradite to isolation.

"It doesn't matter now, does it? That was a lifetime ago. Come to my workshop. I don't trust you to not mess up my babies, and don't touch anything in there either! There's a place in the back of my workshop where you can rest. It's not much, but it'll keep you out of my hair."

"But where you can still keep an eye on us?" I asked, amused.

"This one's smart Bethtizmo. More so than you." The old woman smiled slyly.

"I keep telling you I'm not stupid, Nim." Bethtizmo sighed.

"Then why'd you steal from me if you weren't?" Nim demanded as she walked down a brightly lit corridor without waiting to see if we would follow. What looked like moss coated the walls from floor to ceiling.

"I left you provisions as payment."

"That space garbage?! Dehydrated chemical pouches of toxicity? I thought you were trying to kill me. You're still a stupid thief," she muttered as the hall opened into a workshop. Tools and parts were strewn across a large worktable. Gadgets and parts filled the shelves that lined the room from floor to ceiling. Nim gestured with one arm towards a dirty mattress in the corner as she made space on the worktable.

"And you're an old hag," Bethtizmo mumbled under his breath.

"You really shouldn't have stolen from her, you know," I responded knowing how badly that would have hurt Nim, or any Peradite.

"Desperate times, Esmerelda. She had two accelerators she wasn't using, and I needed one."

"Did you ever just ask her for it?"

"Of course, I did. She said no, but it was just sitting in a pile of junk she had."

"That was her parts stash. You should know how important those are to Peradites."

"That's not how it works, Esmerelda. The knowledge isn't the same for everyone. Some I know just about everything and others, the bare minimum."

"Let me fill you in then. Peradites are born inventors, tinkerers. It's in their blood, as innate as breathing. Even on this rock Nim makes things. I recognize Peradite handiwork all over. She uses her parts stash to create and improve on things, so what you stole was something incredibly valuable to her."

"I thought it was just old junk she was keeping and wouldn't part with because she was a miserable lonely hag." Bethtizmo shifted on the mattress.

"A miserable lonely hag that let you stay here free of charge for weeks? Seems like she was more hospitable than you give her credit for."

Bethtizmo's face reflected his troubled thoughts as he turned away from me.

Claraseve's stomach rumbled loudly and soon mine joined in.

Nim's face appeared. "I can't work with all this noise." Nim glared at us. "The talking and the stomach growling. Follow me and I'll bring you food. Don't touch anything!" she warned.

"We didn't mean to disturb you, Nim. We really can't afford to take a break—" What I wanted to say is we couldn't afford for her to take a break but I knew if I questioned her ability, it would just anger her.

"You need to eat, and I need a break to let my brain think."

We all stood up—except Miswala and Kokshai who were still weak—and followed the short woman, whose lithe movements were at odds with her age, to a small alcove.

"Sit," she demanded, pointing to a small table.

We complied and heard her rummaging around the next room in what had to be the kitchen. Minutes later she came back carrying plates overflowing with different fruits, vegetables, and a type of nut that could only be found on Peradite. I bit into one and groaned in delight as the sweetness slid down my throat.

"How do you grow these here?" I studied the nut and wondered if I could take one to try to propagate on Earth.

"Special lights I built to replicate Peradite's sun," Nim replied shortly.

"You must miss it," Claraseve said.

"Bah, I don't miss anything." She stalked off, ending the conversation.

Bethtizmo looked forlornly at his plate and mumbled, "No meat?"

"Meat is for Neanderthals! Are you a stupid Neanderthal?"

He signed and decided against answering.

"Maybe you're not so stupid after all," Nim cackled from the kitchen.

Claraseve slid her hand onto Bethtizmo's and shook her head as he opened his mouth to retort. Instead, he popped a small green fruit into his mouth and grinned in surprise at its flavor. Before long the plates were empty and bellies full.

"I don't think I have ever been this full of nonmeat substance," Bethtizmo said.

"That's because they're Peradite fruits and vegetables. They enhanced the DNA of the plant to pack as many proteins and nutrients as possible into them," I explained while taking the last nut from the plate.

"How is that even possible?" Claraseve asked.

"Nothing is impossible with a Peradite," I replied.

"Except the impossible," Nim mumbled as she appeared by my elbow and cleared the plates.

"Let me help." I stood, but she brushed off my attempts.

"You'll only annoy me." She disappeared into the kitchen. She came back a short time later and shooed us back into her workshop. Miswala and Kokshai still lay on the mattresses laid out on the floor.

I sat down next to Miswala with a twinge of guilt. We had been eating and filling our bellies while Miswala suffered.

"I'm sorry. We shouldn't have left you."

"It's OK, Merelda. You need to eat, I do not. You've already done so much for us."

I nodded. "Try to get some more rest. It shouldn't be too much longer until we get you back home."

We all watched in silence for the next few hours as Nim worked. She mumbled, scribbled equations, hammered, gathered parts from around the room, lit a torch a few times, and used other tools I had never seen until finally she had two small metal spheres in her hand. I got up as she walked over.

"They're done. Both can either open or close a door. I made them foolproof."

"Nothing's foolproof," Bethtizmo quipped from the ground as he rose up.

"Stupid proof then," Nim replied and held his gaze, only breaking it as alarms blared in every room.

"What is that?" I yelled, at this point really getting tired of hearing alarms.

Nim scrambled over to a screen on the side of the room which showed a familiar ship approaching.

"They've followed you here. You must hurry! Open the door! Hold the orb in your hands and think of that world, and only of that world. Hold the image in your mind and say its name as you throw the orb to the ground. It'll open a door and you can get back home. To close a door, think of that door closed. Got it?" She thrust the orbs into my hand.

"Come with us, Bethtizmo. You can't outrun the grifters this time," I pleaded.

"I have something that can help." Nim nimbly ran up a ladder and grabbed a small box off a shelf before returning. She thrust it into Bethtizmo's hands.

"It's a cloaking device. Attach it to your control panel and it will hide your ship from any sensor. Take it."

The alarms grew louder and more insistent as the ship loomed over them.

"I'm going with Bethtizmo, Esmerelda," Claraseve said suddenly, as if just making up her mind. I saw the stars she loved reflected in her eyes and knew she was going where she belonged.

Bethtizmo grabbed Nim's hands. "Come with us. You can call me stupid every day."

Her gaze softened and she shook her head. Gently, she removed her hands.

"I can't leave my plants. Or my things. It's all I have. Don't worry about me, just go."

"How will—"

"GO!" Nim yelled.

She turned towards me as they ran out of the room to their ship.

"You won't make it out, you know that."

"I'm an old woman who's lived many many years. Now go." She pushed me away.

Gripping the orbs, I said a small prayer to M'ra and imagined Trilesk.

"Think of home, Miswala."

I threw the orb onto the ground and as it shattered a bright light burst from it. I looked up and saw the door stretch open with familiar blue sand on the other side. I approached the door but stopped to look back at Nim.

"Merelda, we need to go through NOW."

I glanced back and saw the door start to shrink. I knew I may never have another chance to ask, but I had to get them home. I lengthened my stride and leapt through the door, landing on the blue sand of Trilesk. I turned back towards the door.

"NIM," I screamed as an explosion threw her to the ground and the door disappeared followed by a whoosh as the air moved in to fill the void.

"MERELDA!" Miswala shouted in alarm.

I looked across the sands and saw Thargon and his men getting ready to breach the other door. They hadn't come through yet! With renewed energy I raced across the sands, orb in hand. At the last minute Thargon looked up and saw me, eyes wide in recognition. His howl of rage was cut off as I threw the orb and it shattered on the sands, slamming the door shut. I stood there for a moment and then the air burst with music from the Trilesks as they surrounded Miswala and Kokshai.

Aslame floated over, a serene smile on their face.

"I told you M'ra had faith in you."

21) Kate's Door

Kate heard the creak of old leather as she shifted in the chair and groaned. She had a new appreciation for what Aunt Esme was capable of. The open journal shifted on her lap, and she glanced down to see —Kate—in flourished lettering, along with *Harrikan?* underneath a watercolor picture of—what was that? Kate peered closer and tried to make out what her aunt had painted. It looked like a small island floating in a sea of stars? Why did that look familiar? A memory tugged and swelled and washed over her as Kate let go.

Eight-year-old Kate skipped down the garden path. Aunt Esme was due back from traveling soon and she wanted to get some flowers for her. Aunt Esme loved flowers and Kate wanted to do something to show her aunt how much she missed her. A path veered off that Kate had never noticed before (which happened sometimes) so she followed it along. She was busy counting steps so wasn't paying as much attention as she should have and one minute she was on the path, the next on the edge of a dark island floating in space, surrounded by what looked like dark waters. She started and looked around, afraid. Her heart hammered in her chest and Kate froze. No, she mustn't be afraid. Aunt Esme had prepared her for this. They had played pretend all summer where they would discover a new world and figure out what Kate had to do. Except, this wasn't pretend. She took a few deep breaths in, like Aunt Esme told her to do when she was in a predicmament, predicanent, predica something and looked around. It was dark out here, with the only light shining from the moons above. Low-lying dwellings dotted the island. Wherever she was, there weren't that many people here. A trilling from behind her made Kate twirl around and she came face to well, face, with a creature her size. Its body was smooth and black with large black eyes. It tilted its head at Kate and trilled. Little Kate wasn't sure what it wanted until it turned and slipped into the sea of stars. Little Kate gasped for several reasons. 1) The creature didn't plummet into space, but instead swam around and beckoned Kate to join with encouraging squeals. 2) Everywhere the creature touched, the water glowed bright blue, like the glowing algae plankton she had learned about in school. 3) Little Kate could see through the water. She saw the creature in the water, swimming, and watched as it dove down and did a somersault before it broke the surface. And with every movement it trailed bright blue glowing. Little Kate was overwhelmed with the beauty of it, but curiosity quickly took over and she too dove into the water. She came up but wasn't wet, and whatever she was swimming in was lighter than water. She heard the creature squeal and turned as they beckoned her to play. For hours they swam in the sea of stars as they chased and turned and did acrobatics until Kate, exhausted, crawled onto land and saw the shimmer of the door. With a wave to her new friend, she turned and went home where she was met by a smiling Aunt Esme.

"I remember. I remember everything." Kate's hand flew to her face as memories of that summer came rushing back. Her mom and aunt yelling and arguing:

"I don't want her to have it, Esmerelda. I don't want her to have anything to do with your family."

"They're your family too, Jani. Please don't do this. She belongs here."

"She belongs to me and my world, the real one, not your delusional

one. She's not coming back here, and I don't want you anywhere near her. I told you in the beginning I didn't want you to expose her to this. I begged you but you were too selfish and self-centered. You couldn't leave it alone. You couldn't leave Kate as she was."

"You can't do that, Jani. She has gifts that run through our family, that make her different. You're being selfish for wanting to shut that part of her life out. Tell me, how selfish was it to use me as a last resort when no one else could watch her?"

"Oh, no, you did not go there. You owed me after everything you've done. You OWED ME to watch your niece for a single NORMAL summer and you couldn't do it. I shouldn't have trusted you—that was my mistake—but I am not letting you ruin Kate's life too. We're leaving. Don't come around again."

"Mommy, no, I want to be with Aunt Esme."

"Your aunt is very sick, Kate. One day you'll understand . . ."

Grief wracked Kate's body as the memory faded. Her aunt had always wanted her; it was her mother that had stopped Kate from coming back or being alone with Aunt Esme. Her mom worked for years to make Kate believe her aunt didn't have time for her and made her believe that nothing from that summer was real. Never again. Her mom had no power over her life, her actions, or her decisions anymore.

A small corner of a blue sheet of paper jutted out from her aunt's stack of papers and caught Kate's attention as she stood. She pulled it from the stack and recognized the drawing from her dream. It was the one her aunt had been studying in her dream that looked like blueprints for a spaceship. This wasn't a coincidence. This had to be where her aunt was being held. With a triumphant cry, she clutched the papers in her fist and hurried down to the kitchen. She had almost reached the kitchen door when the crystal began to whisper again. Her pace slowed as she concentrated, but it was no use. The whispering was too low to make out what was being said. Distracted, she pushed the door open to see Mrs. B and Maggie, along with Mr. H around the table. Kate stood for a moment, not saying a word.

"Are you OK, dear?" Mrs. B asked.

Kate shook her head to clear it and tried to focus. "I'm fine. I just, I remember it all. The entire summer. I remember all the wonderful memories spent here with you, Mrs. B, and pestering you outside in the gardens, Mr. H, but most of all I remember Aunt Esme and the doors." Kate sat down, and the words poured out in a rush.

"That summer I went through a door." Kate paused and looked around at everyone to let it sink in. "Aunt Esme prepared me by playing a game of pretend. We'd play out different scenarios, but all had the same theme: What would I do if I found myself on another planet or different dimension? Genius, really, looking back. She was training me without me even being aware. Anyway, *I* may not have been aware, but my mom was. She found out somehow. Either a slip up on one of our phone calls or a mother's intuition. Somehow, she knew, and she came to check on me. Unfortunately, I was wearing this necklace and my mom somehow recognized it." Kate fingered the crystal and the whispering intensified, yet Kate still couldn't make out any words. She put her hand around the cup of tea Mrs. B had placed before her and continued.

"Aunt Esme had shown it to me earlier in the day. Later on, I snuck into her study. I knew I shouldn't, but the crystal called to me even back then. I knew how to open the safe since I had just watched Aunt Esme do it. I thought I would just wear it for a bit, and put it back without anyone knowing." Guilt washed over her. If she just would have left the crystal alone, her mom never would have found out. Then Kate never would have forgotten the summer, and her aunt would still be safe, not being held somewhere. She stopped her train of thought. No. She knew that wasn't right. This time she wouldn't feel guilty over her actions as an eight-year-old. Nor would she feel guilty over her mom's reaction. She couldn't change the past, and who's to say it wouldn't be worse now? She continued on.

"Unfortunately, my mom walked in when I had it on and she knew everything with one look. I've never seen her so furious. She was so angry at Aunt Esme, and they fought and screamed at each other. In the end she took me away and never let me come back. My mom told me over and over that Aunt Esme left me all summer with the housekeeper and traveled for work. She said she was mad at Aunt Esme for leaving me alone all the time with just my imagination to keep me company. Over time I doubted my memories, and even suppressed them since it hurt to think none of it was real. After that summer I only saw my aunt for birthdays and holidays, but she was never allowed to be alone with me. My mom told me Aunt Esme had mental health issues but wouldn't tell me what. As I got older the visits grew fewer and fewer. I never understood why it hurt so much to see her, and hurt even more when she left. Now I do."

"Wow, I knew your mom was manipulative, but this is a whole other level. Does this mean your mom knew about the other dimensions all along?" Maggie asked, shaking her head in disbelief.

"I'm not sure. She could know things or sense things without knowing exactly what they are. I'll be asking her next time I see her," Kate said then froze, head tilted, forehead furrowed.

"Kate, what is—" Mrs. B started to ask.

"Shhh. Don't you hear that?" Kate concentrated hard on the noise.

"Hear what?" Maggie asked and looked around in confusion.

Kate bolted out of the chair and dashed to the solarium. She halted in the doorway leading in, as the others smacked into her from the sudden stop. A tear appeared a few feet above the floor and grew. Wind—slow at first, then faster and faster as it built up speed—

hurtled objects around the room and thrashed around.

"WHAT IS IT?" Maggie yelled over the roar of the wind as the tear exposed a floor, and then a green foot.

"GET BACK!" Kate yelled, as the tear grew to show Thargon on board a ship.

"AUNT ESME!" Kate's face drained of color as she took in the sight of her aunt in chains, disheveled, clothes in rags, filthy, and bruised. Kate knew it was her, even before she lifted her head. Eyes vacant, they slowly focused on Kate in horror.

Thargon shook the chains that held her aunt.

"The choice is yours. Your descendant or the location of the door? Which will it be?"

"Kate run!" Esmerelda yelled with what little strength she had left.

"You've chosen," Thargon sneered as he edged closer to the tear. His arm reached through as Kate stood rooted to the spot and listened as the chaos progressed around her but underneath, she heard the whispers, louder now, as they told her what to do and say. Words erupted out of her mouth as she repeated what the voices said.

"Myargo clomenta pitha lomar, myargo clomenta pitha lomar, myargo clomenta pitha lomar." Her hands moved on their own and flowed from one movement to the next with ease.

She focused on what the voices were telling her, teaching her, letting them move her. She was subtly aware of shouts on the other side of the tear as the fabric began to mend and shrink. Thargon raged as his prey evaded him again. In desperation he reached through just as the tear closed, and all was silent.

They stood in stunned silence and stared at the green fingers that littered the floor, before Kate flopped to the floor as exhaustion wracked her body.

Mrs. B squatted next to her, concern written on her face. "Are you OK?"

Kate nodded as her mind raced. What had just happened? Did she do that or was it the crystal? She took a few shuddering breaths and felt the strength return to her limbs.

Maggie stared at Kate for a long moment before she spoke. "That crystal glowed, Kate, when you started chanting. It glowed like it was helping you. What is going on?"

Kate stared up at her best friend. "It showed me what to do. Without it, I couldn't have closed that door."

"Is it telling you to do anything right now?" Maggie asked as she eyed the necklace.

"No, it was in the moment, like it wanted to protect me," Kate replied. She stood on shaky legs and wiped her palms on her jeans. "I know you all are just worried, but please trust me. It's not dangerous, at least not to us. It wants to help us. I can feel that, but I don't have any more answers to your questions. You know everything I do. For now let's focus on the fact that we know for certain Thargon has Aunt Esme."

The others looked unconvinced but let their questions go unanswered for now, for which Kate was grateful.

"So how do we go about rescuing Esmerelda? Do you think you could find a door that would lead us to her? I mean, now that you've remembered you're a traveler you should be able to see them, right?" Mrs. B asked.

"In theory, maybe? I've only been through one door so I'm not exactly an expert at spotting them. Plus, I'm not sure if there are doors to spaceships or if it's just other planets. There are some gaps in my knowledge. And say I could find doors. . . . According to Aunt Esme there are hundreds of doors in and around the house. It could take months or years without finding the right one, and Aunt Esme doesn't have that kind of time." Kate gestured for the others to precede her to the kitchen and followed.

When they were settled around the kitchen table Maggie spoke up. "Is there a way we can get those people to help? The ones your aunt wrote about? They would know what we're up against and could help us find your aunt."

"Bethtizmo and Claraseve? That's a good idea. They have knowledge of that dimension and Thargon. Mrs. B, how did Aunt Esme communicate with others in other dimensions?"

"I don't know, Kate. We were never involved in that part of her life. We just took care of the house and the grounds. I'm sorry, love."

"I may have a way," Mr. H spoke up with a sheepish grin. "I've been working on a cross-dimensional communicator in my free time."

"In your free time you've been creating a way to talk to other people in other dimensions? I'm lucky if I have the motivation to do my laundry for the week." Maggie stared wide-eyed.

"What do you need to try to reach them?" Kate asked.

"Do you have any identifiers?"

"Just the name of the ship. The *Teinresy*." Kate remembered seeing it on the side of the ship as Aunt Esme and the others ducked into it.

"I'll go see what I can do. It may be a long shot though," Mr. H said and bowed his head.

"A long shot is better than nothing, Mr. H," Kate said with a grateful smile.

They watched Mr. H leave the room and Kate got up from her chair. "I'm going to grab the journal from the study. It has the location in it to the door of Trilesk, and we can't risk Thargon getting his hands on it. As much as I hate to say it, we have to consider burning it." A sharp pang shot through her heart but Kate knew it would be the right thing to do, no matter how badly she wanted to keep it for herself. If Thargon got that location, there would be no end to his power, along with the demise of worlds. No, it had to be done. Kate strode back to the study, pushed the door open, walked in, and stopped in the middle of the room.

"Hello, Mother. What are you doing here?"

22) Kidnapping

Her mom looked up from where she sat in the leather chair behind the desk.

"I thought I would find you here even though I expressly forbid it."

"You did, but that was before. We found evidence that Aunt Esme's alive. You can't take this house from her now."

"Still going on about that? And where is she? In the closet? Behind the door? In a mental institution maybe?"

"No, and you wouldn't understand, but she *is* alive, so you need to call everything off."

"I'm afraid I can't do that, Kate. I have court in two days and a buyer lined up. This house is going to be torn down to make room for shiny new condos."

"You can't do that! She's alive and this is HER house, MY house!"

"It's my house too, Kate, even if my mom left it to Esmerelda. Don't forget I was raised here."

"Mom, you can't. She's alive!" Kate drew herself up and faced her mom. She wouldn't back down this time.

"And again, where is she?" her mom asked from her seat.

"You wouldn't understand."

"No? Try me. Talk to me, Kate. You've pulled away since the day you came back here. This house is not healthy for you, and your aunt was mentally unstable. She drew you into her world when you were eight. She made up stories until she actually believed them. She couldn't handle the real world, so she created a fantasy one here. You started to believe her lies and that's when I had to take you away and limit your exposure to her. I let her be because she wasn't hurting anyone in this old house, but I kept you away for your protection."

"What if her world wasn't made-up?"

"See! This is why I was worried! Her world isn't real, Kate. This isn't healthy. Your mental health was always more fragile after your exposure to her and her fantasies."

"It wasn't fragile, Mom, and Aunt Esme wasn't unstable. Her reality was real. There's more than this world, like the one we came from."

"We came from here, Kate! There's nothing special or different about us. I did the genealogy when she first spouted this nonsense. I followed our family back five hundred years, so no, our family isn't from some other world. Our family is firmly planted in THIS one, the REAL one. Kate, please, you need help. Let me help you. There's a place where you can rest and talk to someone."

"I've seen things you can't explain, and you can't convince me that I'm losing my mind. I'm not that little girl anymore."

"Kate, please, you aren't seeing what you think you're seeing. It's all in your mind."

"What about Mrs. B and Mr. H? They can tell you what's going on, or ask Maggie, she's seen things as well."

"Honey, there's no one else here. Maggie's back at the apartment. She's the one who told me you weren't returning her calls or texts either, which had her worried. And there's never been a Mrs. B or Mr. H, ever. It's always just been your aunt here in the house."

"That's impossible! Just let me get them."

"Kate! They aren't real, none of this is real. You're sick and you need help. Let me help you, please."

"Mom, I'm not sick, just let me get them!"

"I can't let you do that. I can't let you continue. It's time to bring you home, back to the real world."

Kate felt a sharp pain in her arm and looked up to see her Dad holding a syringe. She had been so engrossed in her argument she didn't hear him come up behind her. He must've been hiding behind the door. She turned to face him, and he caught her just as she fell.

"I'm sorry, Kate, but this is for your own good," her mom said as the world spun into blackness.

Kate drifted calmly through a haze of smoke as the necklace whispered to her. It wanted to show her something, something she needed to see. The smoke cleared and Kate saw people, *her people,* in all walks of life—laughing, walking in pairs along pathways through exotic-looking greenery, singing, living their daily lives. Everyone looked so happy, and content. She felt the overwhelming joy her people had at being alive. It was a utopia. The vision shifted and she was shown a handful of Eronians, wearing cloaks and carrying things. *Travelers*, Kate thought, but one stood out. It was the way she carried herself and the way others deferred to her. Kate took in the woman's features, so like Kate's and she wondered if this was an ancestor. *Harrikan*, the necklace whispered. Born with the rare ability to open doors, not just find them. Rarer than rare.

The vision darkened and people were running in fear, screaming as they were shot down in the streets by large armed creatures. Smoke hung in the air as the same creatures set fire to all the buildings, not content with massacring her people. The point of view changed, and she glimpsed a father barring the door against more armed creatures as they approached, yelling at the woman, the *Harrikan,* in the center of the room to hurry, as her hands moved frantically. Off to the side two young girls gripped each other, the oldest shushing her younger sister's cries.

The vision split: one side showed the family, and the other side showed a large imposing creature in the caverns below the city. The crystal whispered his name, *Rahsh,* and fury washed over her, and she knew he was to blame for all this destruction. It was his greed for the orange crystals—abundant on Eronia and so valuable and rare elsewhere. Her breath caught as Rahsh discovered a large crystal, embedded in the cavern wall where it had stood for eons. Couldn't the soldiers feel the awareness of the crystal? Didn't they know how sacred it was? Her people worshipped it, worshipped Akashte. Akashte. It knew what was happening to her people and knew what was about to happen. Why couldn't Rahsh feel the energy held in the crystal, the awareness, or the other soldiers? How could they be so oblivious? Rahsh barked orders for the crystal to be dug out, and became enraged when it wouldn't budge, despite his strongest soldier's efforts. He snarled and a weapon was wheeled in and aimed at Akashte. Within moments a white hot, laser beam began cutting the rock surrounding the crystal. It didn't get far as the energy was absorbed by Akashte. Blinded by greed, Rahsh pushed the lever, increasing the intensity to no avail. In a blind fury, Rahsh grabbed the weapon, strode towards Akashte, and pulled the lever all the way. Even though Kate knew this had already happened, she prayed for a different outcome. Akashte exploded just as the frenzied mother jumped through the door with her children, and a piece of Akashte attached itself to the Harrikan's crystal and began to glow, just as the vision faded.

The crushing grief of her people crippled her, and Kate lay on the ground and sobbed. The grief slowly let up and she became aware of the voices as they showed her the way to become a Harrikan. The crystal, silenced for generations, vibrated softly and Akashte wrapped her in love and told her all the secrets it held.

Kate came to slowly and struggled to open her eyes amid the pounding in her head. She groaned and heard an unfamiliar male voice in the background. "She's waking up."

The edge of the bed dipped as someone sat down next to her and held her wrist.

"Heart rate is back to normal. Kate, can you hear me? Do you know where you are?"

Kate shook her head and fought the nausea that struck her.

"You need to lie still. I'm going to give you something for the nausea."

"Headache," Kate replied through thick lips.

"I can give you something for the headache too."

Kate struggled to remember what happened and groaned at her pounding head.

"Dad."

"I'm here, Kate," her dad replied, and the other side of the bed dipped as he sat down. Kate tugged on the restraints holding her wrists and legs down.

"Shhh, don't struggle. I'm sorry about the restraints, but we can't risk you running away. You need help, more than we can give." He stopped, words choked by tears she couldn't see and heard the anguish in his voice.

"Water."

"Of course." The faucet turned on and then off and a few minutes later she felt a straw on her bottom lip. She greedily sucked water into her parched mouth until her dad took it away.

"Easy now. I don't want you throwing it all up."

Kate forced her eyes open, lifted her head, and surveyed the room.

It was a typical hourly motel room, complete with a stained ceiling. She watched a centipede crawl across the patch and prayed its legs would hold it up there. Two men stood watch in front of the door.

"They're here to help get you to the center. We had to stop because you reacted badly to the sedative."

"You kidnapped me against my will. This is illegal!"

"You forced us to this extreme. You aren't yourself, and you're seeing things, which makes you a danger to yourself."

"I'm not seeing things, Dad. They're real! If you would just untie me, I could show you."

"Nice try, kiddo. I'm not untying you."

"Dad, please, you know me, you need to trust me. Mom's the one who's lost it over Aunt Esme and her house. There are things you don't understand."

"I understand you need help. I understand your mom and I want what's best for you, and right now that's the center. They can help you there."

"You don't know what's best for me; you've always let Mom run the show and you just go along with it. I finally stood up to Mom, and now you think I'm losing my grip on reality when I've never been more sure of anything in my life! I KNOW what I saw was real and no amount of time in a 'center' will convince me otherwise. Please. Aunt Esme's still alive and if I don't stop Mom I don't know if I'll ever be able to help her get back."

"Hey, Mr. Jones, we're gonna go get some coffee from across the street. Do you want anything?" asked one of the men standing guard.

"Is it a good idea for you to leave?" her dad asked the men.

"Her vitals are stable, and it's a long trip ahead, so yeah."

"Then no, I'm fine, thanks."

The men left and Kate's mind fought to find an escape."

"It won't work. Whatever you think you can do, you can't escape.

You may as well resign yourself to this and stop fighting."

"Wasn't it you and Mom who taught me to fight for what I believe in? Or was that only when it was what you believed in too? What if I start screaming? How would you explain this to the police?"

"I have court papers, Kate. The front desk's been informed of our situation and won't call the police. Even if they did call, the police can't do anything."

The conversation was interrupted by the ringing of the hotel phone. Her dad grabbed the receiver and listened to the other end.

"What do you mean you need me to come down? It's not my fault your system crashed. Can I just give you my credit card info over the phone? Fine, I'll be right down." Her dad stood up and spoke quietly.

"I have to go to the front office. While I'm gone don't scream. If you do, we'll have to quiet you. It's for your own good. We're trying to get you the help you need." He leaned over, kissed her forehead, and smoothed a stray hair. "I love you," he whispered and left the room.

A minute later the door opened up and Maggie scurried over to the bed and tugged at the restraints.

"Oh, Jesus, Kate! What did they do to you? We have to hurry. Your dad's gonna figure out something's wrong when the front desk has no clue about the system crash."

"That was you? How did you find me?"

"I saw a couple of men carrying you to a van with your parents and I followed. When those two guys left, I knew I had to do something. Now let's get out of here." The last of the restraints fell away and Kate stood up, but it was too late. The door opened and both men strode in. They looked at Kate and Maggie and blocked the door.

"What's going on here, ladies?"

"I came in to clean the room and saw her tied up, so I let her loose. I don't want any trouble."

"This doesn't concern you, so leave."

Maggie put her head down and moved towards the door. She approached the men, eyes averted.

They moved out of the way for her to pass and before they could react, she brought a can of pepper spray up and sprayed them in the face. They screamed and dropped to the floor as they pawed at their eyes.

"C'MON, KATE!" Maggie yelled just as her dad reappeared in the doorway.

"Well-played, Maggie. Now, why don't you drop the pepper spray and back up?"

Maggie stepped over the men who writhed in pain on the floor.

"Why don't you two go run water on your eyes?" her dad directed towards the men on the floor. They got up and stumbled to the bathroom.

"I'm sorry, Dad, but I don't have time for this. Aunt Esme's running out of time, and you're so wrapped up in what Mom says you can't stop to think that what I may be saying is true. So, I guess I'll just have to show you."

Kate reached for Maggie's hand and pulled her to her side. The voices grew louder and she welcomed them as she stood in her full glory, the last Harrikan. She finally understood who she was and where she had come from.

"Mehera Golana Puchuty. Mehera Golana Puchuty. Mehera Golana Puchuty."

"Kate, I don't know what you're doing but it won't work."

"You'll see soon enough, Dad."

Kate's hands moved, and she could see the energy, all the energy, in the room. Some moved and flowed like water, some hovered, some emitted from the people, others from objects in the room. Everything had energy. Everything, and it was beautiful, and made sense, and

Kate's heart soared with the possibilities. The voices continued as they showed her what to do: how to move the energy, change it with her hands, and use it to do what she wanted. She gathered it around her and focused on opening a door.

"Kate, stop this!" Her dad's eyes bulged as a hole appeared in the room.

Wind whipped at Kate's hair, but she stood confident and powerful. She continued chanting and Aunt Esme's house appeared on the other side of the hole.

She looked at her father. "I love you, Dad, but I'm going back to save Aunt Esme. Don't follow me."

Her dad's legs gave out and he crumpled to the ground. Kate felt sorry for him, caught up in his wife's lies. Her mother had a lot to answer for.

"Ready?" Kate asked Maggie.

"Always," Maggie replied, and they both stepped through.

23) The Showdown

Kate blinked in the bright sunlight as she and Maggie stepped onto her aunt's front lawn. A moving truck was parked in the drive. Loud voices carried through the open front door. Kate and Maggie came closer and heard Mrs. B's raised voice. Kate looked at Maggie and raised her eyebrows. She had never heard Mrs. B raise her voice before.

"Esmerelda never would have given you this house! Never!" Mrs. B shouted.

"I have the deed to the house with her signature that says otherwise. Now, you and anyone else in here had better pack your things and get out before I call the police and have you removed!" her mom shouted back.

"Kate won't let you, the house won't let you, and we won't let you."

"Kate's on her way to forget about you, this house, everything, especially Esmerelda!"

"I won't forget, Mom," Kate spoke from the open door, Maggie right behind. "You drugged me, and kidnapped me, and were going to send me to a facility to try to make me think I was losing my mind. You were going to try to make me forget *again*. You're so obsessed with destroying this house and Aunt Esme that you've destroyed our relationship. I'm done listening to you." Kate channeled the anger, hurt, and betrayal and used it to give her strength.

"Kate." Her mom tried to hide her surprise. "Honey, I'm not sure what's going on with you, but why don't we talk about it somewhere private?"

"No. I'm done listening to you. This house is mine. I won't let you destroy it." Kate faced her mom, calm and unflinching for the first time in their relationship.

"She said Esmerelda signed the house over to her over a year ago, Kate." Mrs. B joined Maggie behind Kate.

"It should be easy to prove it's forged, and if it is you'd be disbarred, right, Mom? I mean, you know the law better than I do," Kate said and tilted her head thoughtfully as her eyes held her mom's.

"You don't know what you're talking about." Her mom looked away and Kate knew she was right. Kate pushed on.

"You wanted to punish Aunt Esme, but this isn't the way. This won't make you feel better. It's not Aunt Esme's fault you couldn't find the doors." Kate held her ground.

"Kate, sweetheart, I don't know what you're talking about but your aunt wasn't well." Her mom moved to put her hand on Kate's shoulder but froze as Kate began to talk.

"I remember everything. I remember your fight with Aunt Esme. You told her I wouldn't be part of her world. I remember how furious you were that I traveled through a door. You knew about the doors. You've known all this time. You were going to cart me off to a center and make me think I was losing my mind. That I dreamt this all up in my head."

Her mom's face drained of color as Kate's words sunk in. "Honey, please, let's talk rationally. There are no doors, no other dimensions or universes, just ours."

"No, Mom, there are so many worlds out there, and Aunt Esme

is stuck in one, trapped and in serious danger. I'm not going to be pushed around or manipulated by you anymore." Kate fixed her mom with an unwavering stare and continued. "Here's what you're going to do. You're going to call your lawyer and drop the case and call the developer and tell him you can't sell him the property. You're a lawyer. Tell them what you have to do to make the whole thing stop."

"Kate, please." Her mom's voice rose an octave, which is when Kate usually caved.

"Not this time, Mom. I'm done pretending to be somebody I'm not to live up to your expectations. This house and everyone in it are a huge part of my life. I won't let you take that away from me." Kate tilted her head at her mom. "Or do you need proof that there are other doors? I can open them, Mom, right here in the living room if you need proof. Just ask Dad. Oh, you may have some explaining to do when you get home."

Her mom's shoulders slumped and for a moment she looked like a lost little girl. "This is a mistake, Kate. One I hope never comes back to bite you."

It took less time than Kate thought to send the movers away and for her mom to make the necessary phone calls. She hung up with the last lawyer and turned to Kate. "What now?"

"That's up to you. You can leave and go back to your perfectly normal life," Kate replied. It was hard to believe that she had won against her mom. She had never been more proud of herself and resisted the urge to dance around the parlor.

"Will you still be in it?" her mom asked, and Kate was surprised to see tears before her mom blinked rapidly to get rid of them.

"That depends on you. I won't be manipulated anymore and it'll take a long time to work through the damage you've caused."

"I see." Her mom looked out the window and stood in silence for a moment. Mrs. B motioned towards the kitchen as she and Maggie left. They knew there was no threat from my mom anymore.

"I haven't been in this house since I was seventeen. It's smaller than I remember," her mom mused. She shivered and asked, "Do you know what you're getting yourself into choosing this life? It's dangerous."

"I can handle danger."

"You have no idea what danger truly is. The danger out there with those doors—" her mom's voice trailed off and she shuddered, eyes downcast. Her voice sounded small and timid, like a child's. "There are dark doors, Kate. Dark ones, with dark things looking to eat the light from ours. I went through a door once, only once, and never again." Her mom shivered more and wrapped her arms around herself as her teeth chattered, even decades later at what she had seen.

"Tell me what happened," Kate said firmly. Something told her she needed to hear this. Her mom looked up at her in surprise and then gave in.

"I knew something was different about my mom and Esmerelda. They would walk into a closet yet disappear when I followed and come back hours later through a room I had just left. Or they would walk through the gardens, and I swear I was right behind them when they would turn a corner and vanish. I was so jealous of her, Kate, jealous of her time with my mom, jealous of their relationship, jealous of the happiness I saw in their eyes every time they left home. I became determined to join them, instead of always being left behind with Mrs. B. I just wanted to be included, to feel like I mattered."

Her mom blew out air before continuing. "It was a beautiful summer day, hot and sunny. I watched and waited for them to leave. I thought if I could just follow them close enough to see where they went, I could follow. I had this grand vision of surprising them and my mom picking me up and twirling me around like she did Esmerelda. I thought we could be a family again. Sure enough, my mom called

Esmerelda to bring her pack and they went outside to the garden. They walked through a patch of snapdragons and were gone, puff, just like that. I ran after them and through that patch over and over again, but it wouldn't work for me. I got so angry, Kate. So angry and sad and full of dark thoughts that I couldn't keep it in and when I turned around, I stepped into a world of such complete blackness, so dark you couldn't even see your hand in front of your face. I heard things in that darkness. Slithering, rustling, skittering noises. I was so scared. I knew if I screamed horrible things would happen to me so I bit my hand until I tasted blood, then thought, what if they could smell blood. I started crying, frozen, not wanting to move for fear of running right into whatever was out there. And then I felt it, Kate. It touched me and I swear to God I felt coldness deep in my soul as it started to spread. I turned around and around, desperate to find a way back home and forget anything like this ever existed. I'm not even sure how I escaped. Mrs. B found me in the field, unconscious. I didn't wake up for three days and I never told a soul what I went through. Nightmares followed me for years, and once in a while I still wake up in a sweat, biting my hand. Anything to do with doors, I pushed down a deep hole in my mind where it could never see the light of day again. After that, my relationships with my mom and sister suffered and I had no one. Can you imagine being all alone at that age, Kate? Of course not, I made sure you would never feel that way. After my mom died, she left Esmerelda everything: the house, the money, all of it. I begged her to sell the house I despised but she refused. I wanted us to start a new life, in a new house, and actually be sisters, but I knew she would pick traveling over me and this house. This damn house. I wanted it to rot away to nothing.

"That summer I didn't want to leave you here, but I had no one else to turn to. No one else to help. So, you came. And the nightmares started again, and it all came flooding back. The thought of you going where I went nearly drove me mad. I just wanted to protect you. That morning something told me to come and check on you, a feeling that you were in danger. So, I drove here, and when I arrived, you were wearing that necklace. I knew what it meant. I was so angry, angrier than I have been in a long time, and your aunt and I fought. I accused her of things, and she accused me of things, and it got ugly. I took you away and told her she would never see you again. Your father calmed me down and talked me into letting her see you on holidays and birthdays, but I kept a tight watch when she was over. Your father never knew. I never told him what happened with this house, my family, that summer, none of it. I was afraid he would leave me and take you. It sounded crazy even to me and I had lived through it. So, you see, I really was trying to protect you."

Kate replied, "Maybe you were trying to protect me. Maybe you thought if the house was razed, no one would stumble through that horrible door, but did you ever stop to think that the doors would still be there even after the new construction? Who's to say the doors would disappear with the house? The house is special, but only because of the energy it absorbed. If the house was razed, the energy would still be there. If those condos had been built, you'd have potentially hundreds of people who might wander through one."

Her mom's face turned pale. "I never thought of that. I thought once the house was gone, it would all be gone."

"Why didn't you tell your mom or Aunt Esme what happened?" Kate asked.

"I couldn't. They were always gone, leaving me behind. I just wanted to have my family back and it made it worse."

"I think once we rescue Aunt Esme, you should tell her everything. There's a chance you can still save that relationship too. Just promise me, no more secrets between us. They've done enough damage."

Her mom grabbed Kate in a tight hug. "I promise. I love you, Kate. I've only ever wanted to protect you and give you a stable, good life." Her mom let go and looked at Kate. "Now what?"

"You can leave and go home if you want. No one would blame you for it." Kate looked at her mom and continued. "But I'm going to rescue Aunt Esme."

"Why does she need to be rescued? She's capable of taking care of herself. In fact, she's the most capable person I know."

"She's being held captive in another dimension by something," Kate replied gently.

"And what? You're going to go off and rescue her with no training or experience? Your aunt was a seasoned—"

"Is," Kate corrected her mom.

"Is a seasoned traveler with decades of experience. If she got herself captured, what chance do you have?" her mom asked, all pretense gone.

"One I'm willing to take."

Her mom studied Kate's face, set in determination, and seemed to make up her mind. "Then I'm staying."

Kate scrutinized her mom for a moment and then nodded. "OK. But you need to follow my lead on this. No arguments, no questioning me, no manipulations to get me to do what you want. If I sense any of that I will open a door back here and send you through. This is too important for any shenanigans. Deal?" Kate waited for her mom's nod of assent before she continued. "Good. The others are waiting for us, so let's go."

24) Reconciliation

Maggie and Mrs. B broke off their conversation as Kate and her mom entered the room. Maggie cocked an eyebrow at Kate and looked over at Kate's mom with a tilt of her head. Kate knew what her best friend was thinking but pushed on.

"She's staying. She wants to help Aunt Esme? *AND*"- Kate held up a hand - "she understands she has to listen to everything I say, otherwise she'll be sent back home. She also understands what's at risk here, including broken relationships."

"Look, I know I'm not everyone's favorite at the moment."

Maggie scoffed and rolled her eyes while Mrs. B sat, thin-lipped.

Her mom continued, "BUT there are reasons I did what I did, which I've told Kate about. I know I have a lot of issues with this house and my sister, but the bottom line is I love my daughter and would do anything for her. And if my sister is in danger, I want to help."

Kate ignored the looks from Maggie and Mrs. B and gestured for her mom to sit. She briefly filled her mom in, as her mom focused on the kitchen table, not saying a word.

"I think you broke your mom," Maggie whispered to Kate when she finished. Kate shook her head slightly. Maggie might be right but Kate didn't have the time or inclination to sugar-coat things with her mom. Things were happening —like the subtle change of energy in the house, or the way the hairs on the back of her neck stood up— and Kate knew it meant everything was coming to a head.

"I guess you really don't need my protection," her mom replied, ashen.

"I wish I could give you more time to absorb this—" Kate held her mom's eyes.

"But we don't have time. I'll be fine, Kate. Go on." Her mom's voice shook.

Kate turned towards Mrs. B. "Do you still have the papers I gave you earlier?"

Mrs. B got up, opened a cabinet drawer, and pulled them out. "I put them off to the side so they wouldn't get tea on them."

With a grateful smile, Kate took the papers from Mrs. B and smoothed them down on the table. "I think this might be Thargon's ship," she said and pointed to the drawing of a ship's schematics.

"What makes you think that?" Maggie asked.

"Things in this house aren't coincidental. I've dreamt of Aunt Esme and she had them in her hands, studying them. The journal was all about Aunt Esme rescuing Miswala and Thargon's plans for their energy. Thargon somehow opened a door here and if it wasn't for Dasme and Flora, we wouldn't be having this conversation. I've had visions of Aunt Esme chained up somewhere and everything is telling me she's on his ship, *this* ship." Kate thrust a finger at the schematics.

"Let's say we agree it's Thargon's ship, how are we possibly going to find my sister in all that? It's immense!" Kate's mom argued.

"I know. I don't even know what half of these things mean since I've never been on board a spaceship, but it's the only lead we have right now." Kate chewed the corner of her thumb. "We really need to talk to Bethtizmo or Claraseve. They would know what all this means and the most likely spots where they'd be holding her. Without them, I'm just guessing."

"It's done," Mr. H piped up as he walked in from the back door.

"Mr. H! Were you able to reach them?" Kate held her breath and crossed her fingers.

"Maybe. It's like an intergalactic game of telephone and my invention is crude at best. It may take a day or two, so we'll just have to wait and see."

"And we can't even be sure they'll get the messages." Kate's face puckered.

"I wish I had a more definitive answer for you, Kate," Mr. H replied.

"What's our next step?" Maggie asked as everyone looked to her for their next move.

"Next? I think we need to gather everyone and brainstorm ideas. We need to come up with a plan in case Mr. H's message doesn't get through." Kate hoped that wasn't the case. They had a better chance of succeeding with their help. *Hold on, Aunt Esme. Please hold on.*

"I'll get the others and fill them in," Mr. H volunteered and broke Kate's reverie.

"Others?" her mom asked.

"You'll meet them soon enough," Kate said and picked up the papers to study them again, but it was no use. The plans were immense and written in a language she couldn't understand. Her aunt could be held anywhere.

Some time later Mr. H came in followed by Dasme, Flora, Chirp, and Miss Luna.

Kate pulled at the bottom of her lip as everyone settled in and then dove in without any preamble. "Aunt Esme's being held captive on Thargon's ship. The same Thargon that came through a door the other day so we need to figure out a way to save her. She's alive but just barely and I don't know how much longer she can hold out. I think he's trying to get information from her. Information that would lead to weapons so powerful it would make Thargon unstoppable, and no dimension would be safe from him." Kate held up the paper with the drawing. "I think this is his ship's schematics, but we don't know where she's being held, and it's a massive ship. We have a message out to some others we think can help, but we don't know if they received the message."

"So, you have a pile of think, is that it?" Dasme snorted.

"You always were a pessimist." Flora glared at Dasme.

"How is it being a pessimist when I'm just being honest and saying what everyone thinks?" Dasme huffed.

Kate's voice rose above theirs. "We don't have time for your bickering! Aunt Esme's life depends on us, as well as the fate of the worlds! I'm doing the best I can but if you have any other solutions, I'd be glad to hear them."

"Maybe we can help," a strange voice called from the doorway.

A teal man and a raven-haired woman stood in the doorway. "Bethtizmo and Claraseve! You got our message!" Kate cried out in relief.

"If you mean the very garbled, cryptic message, then yes, we got it. Wasn't sure what it meant but we made out Esmerelda's name so thought we better come," Bethtizmo looked everyone over. "I think some introductions are in order since we seem to be at a disadvantage. You know our names, but we don't know you or what we're doing here."

Kate gestured at each person as she introduced them.

"Dasme, Flora, Miss Luna, and Chirp."

"Floranare, Ctonaese, and Drapel." Bethtizmo stated their origins as they nodded in agreement.

Kate pointed out Mrs. B, "Mrs. B."

"Ornabee," Bethtizmo said with a bow. "Esmerelda's mentioned you a time or two. It's a pleasure to meet you." Mrs. B buzzed with pleasure for a moment before getting control of herself.

"Mr. H. He's the one who invented the amazing machine to get you the message." Mr. H nodded his head at Kate's words and flushed.

"Jarnovial with a hint of Peradite. Interesting," Bethtizmo mused.

"Maggie," Kate continued.

"Earth"

"My mother, Janice."

"Sister of Esmerelda, Eronian." Bethtizmo eyed Janice warily and Kate hid a smile. It looked like her aunt may have mentioned her a time or two as well. She shook her head and continued. "And I'm Kate."

"Niece of Esmerelda, daughter of Eronia, last Harrikan and key to the worlds," Bethtizmo said and bowed deeply down before her.

Kate lifted Bethtizmo up by the arm and tried to gain control of her jumbled thoughts. "You really don't need to do that," she said as a swarm of butterflies set off in her stomach.

His eyes searched hers. "You have no idea what power you hold do you?"

"I'm beginning to find out," she murmured, then louder, "I'm glad you're both here. We need your help. I'm afraid Thargon has Aunt Esme aboard his spaceship." Both Bethtizmo and Claraseve hissed and looked surprised. "We have these, but need you to tell us if this is Thargon's ship." Kate gestured towards the papers she had found on her aunt's desk. Claraseve and Bethtizmo crowded around the table and examined the ship's schematics.

"What in the worlds was she doing with this?" Claraseve asked under her breath.

"Is it Thargon's?" Kate asked as the corner of her thumb found its way to her lips again.

"It is. He built a fleet of them that he's used to either conquer or destroy worlds, and he doesn't seem to care which."

Kate's face darkened. All those lives lost. "Why hasn't anyone tried to stop him?"

"Many have. He angered the most powerful Progos from across the galaxy and they sent the best assassins, ships, and mercenaries money could buy, but all failed. He's always been one step ahead of everyone and he thinks he's unstoppable. He was always very arrogant," Claraseve replied. "Which brings me to ask . . . do you have a plan? Thargon won't let any ship get near him. He shoots first, never mind asking questions. How do you plan to get on board when everyone else has failed?"

Kate exhaled sharply and met Claraseve's gaze. "I'm going to open a door. I've done it once before and I know I can do it again. I just need to know *where* on the ship to open one."

"Well, now, that does make things easier for us. This might work. We can use Thargon's arrogance to our advantage. He'll never expect us to just walk in and grab her, so we'll have the element of surprise on our side. We just might actually be able to pull this off," Claraseve smiled at Kate.

Bethtizmo pointed to the lower decks on the schematics. "Esmerelda's most likely being held here in the lower decks."

"Last time we saw her, she was on some kind of deck with Thargon," Kate countered.

"What do you mean, the last time you saw her?" Bethtizmo demanded.

Kate launched into a quick recap. When she was done Bethtizmo whistled in appreciation.

"Even so, he won't keep her there all the time," Bethtizmo said. "She'll be in the way on the bridge, and he won't worry about her escaping because she's too weak. Trust me, most of the time she'll be in the holding cells which are at the lower level."

Kate nodded. "OK. I'll open a door to the holding cells, we'll go through, break Aunt Esme out, and get back here, all before Thargon has any idea we are even there."

"Easy peasy?" Maggie asked.

"Easy peasy." Kate replied with more confidence than she felt. This had to work.

"The next thing we need to decide is who is staying, and who is going." Claraseve spoke to Kate as if she was in charge. With a start she realized she was, and the thought terrified her. What if she failed again? Kate pushed the doubts away. She was a Harrikan. She had help from amazing, resourceful people and the crystal. She wouldn't fail.

"Mr. H and Mrs. B will stay here with Flora, Dasme, Chirp, and Miss Luna."

"I am most certainly not staying behind while Esmerelda perishes aboard the monster's ship. We defeated him once, we can again," Dasme exclaimed and jumped up, brandishing his staff.

Kate turned to Dasme. "You and Flora were very brave, but I need you here to protect this home. We can't have Thargon getting through. It's crucial." Dasme harrumphed, slightly mollified.

"Mom, Maggie, this is going to be extremely dangerous, and I can't guarantee you won't get hurt or worse. I can't ask you to come with me."

"I'm going," they both replied in unison without hesitation. Kate nodded and shifted her attention to Bethtizmo and Claraseve. "We're going to need weapons. Any idea where we can get some?"

Bethtizmo nodded. "We may have brought extra. Weren't sure what we would be walking into." He left and came back into the room carrying two bags.

"That's enough to start a small war," her mom murmured.

Bethtizmo put the bags on the table as Kate cleared it. "You can never be too prepared, especially with what we deal with," he said.

Claraseve opened the bags and inspected the weapons inside. "I'm assuming you haven't used weapons before. Kate?"

Kate held up both hands. "I'll need my hands free."

"You still need one. You can keep it in the holster, but I want everyone armed." Claraseve handed Kate and Maggie small, petite weapons. "These you just point and shoot."

Maggie turned over the weapon that fit in the palm of her hand. "They're awfully small. Does it need bullets?"

"Be careful with that and don't get caught up in size. Those are powerful," Claraseve replied "And no, it doesn't use bullets. Like I said, just point and shoot when the time comes."

"We'll take care of the guards." Bethtizmo gestured towards himself and Claraseve. Kate nodded, grateful to have their expertise and experience. It made her feel like they could actually do this and get back in one piece.

"Mom and Maggie, you'll have to help Aunt Esme out. She looked really weak and I'm not sure she can stand. I'll need to stay focused on keeping the door open."

"Why can't you just open it and leave it?" Claraseve asked. "We've used plenty of doors that have remained open for years."

"Those are naturally created doors. When you open an unnatural door, nature will fight hard to close it, which is why I need to stay focused on keeping it open."

"Can't you just open a new one if it closes?" Maggie asked.

"It takes a few minutes, and what if we're discovered and don't have that time?"

"Point taken."

"Are there any more questions? No? Then let's go bring Aunt Esme home."

25) The Rescue

Everyone grabbed their weapons and headed to the solarium, where, after much discussion, they decided was the best place to open the door.

"Things get noisy when I start, so be prepared."

Kate closed her eyes and pictured the holding cells in Thargon's ship. The desire to get her aunt home and safe consumed her and the voices responded and showed her the way.

"Kilar mondor sophie. Kilar mondor sophie. Kli lemifascia gor. KLI LEMIFASCIA GOR. **KLI LEMIFASCIA GOR!**"

Kate's hands dipped and wove as sparks sizzled from her fingertips. A rip appeared, small at first but steadily grew larger as wind whipped through the room. At first a dingy grey floor appeared, followed by two pairs of purple webbed feet attached to two soldiers with slack jaws at the spectacle before them. Before they could raise either their weapons or an alarm, they toppled over as Claraseve and Bethtizmo fired their weapons.

Maggie nodded in approval and glanced at Bethtizmo and Claraseve.

Claraseve shrugged nonchalantly as Bethtizmo's curt voice carried above the din. "Let's go!"

One by one they stepped through and were met with row after

row of empty cells. Unease crept over Kate as she looked at the rows of cells, far more than were on the schematics.

"We'll start from the right and make our way down. She has to be in one of them," Bethtizmo said as his eyes swept the area.

"There weren't supposed to be this many," Kate's mom said and looked worried.

"I know, but we don't have a choice." Kate moved forward down the first corridor as the others followed, past empty cell after empty cell. The next corridor was the same and the next. Their unease grew with each vacant cell.

"This doesn't feel right," Claraseve said right as the sounds of fighting echoed down the passageway.

"The door!" Kate's heart jumped and she ran down the corridor, followed closely by the others. She slowed her steps as they approached a crossway and hugged the walls. She peered around the corner and jerked her head back.

"What did you see?"

"Thargon's men. Lots of them. They've barricaded themselves in and they're trying to get past the others."

"How did they even know about the door?" Maggie asked as her voice trembled.

"I don't know. Thargon couldn't have anticipated this." Bethtizmo's forehead furrowed.

"No? Then tell me why my aunt's not down here and Thargon's men are? Because it certainly feels like he anticipated this."

Claraseve grabbed Kate's arms and held her gaze. "You need to close the door."

"CHIRP," a thunderous voice boomed.

"What was that?" her mom asked, huddled next to Maggie.

Kate peered around the corner again before she pulled back with a grin.

"I didn't know he could get that big."

The others peered around just in time to see a pair of feet slide down Chirp's throat as Thargon's men retreated back behind the barricade.

"Looks like Chirp has everything under control," her mom said, wide-eyed.

"Not for long," Claraseve said as a film of sweat broke out over her brow.

Kate's breath caught when she saw Thargon, holding a limp woman in his grasp.

"Aunt Esme," she whispered.

Thargon strode to the front of the barricade and barked an order. One of his men handed him a large weapon which Thargon aimed at Chirp, who ducked back through the door just as it slammed shut. Thargon's scream of frustration echoed through the lower levels.

Claraseve pulled Kate back gently as her arms dropped to her sides.

"I couldn't risk them getting through," Kate whispered. She just hoped they had the time for her to make a new door home when the time came.

"We need to move," Bethtizmo replied tersely.

They followed as he raced down the corridor and heard Thargon yell at his men, "I want whoever opened that door found and I want them alive!"

Kate and the others ran until they collapsed against the wall and gasped for air.

Her mom managed to spit out words between gasps. "We . . . need . . . a plan. . . . We . . . can't . . . keep running."

"We need to get to the bridge and save Aunt Esme. If he's keeping her by his side, that's where they'll be going." Kate held her side as a stitch developed and vowed to work on her endurance once she got back home. For now she would just have to push past the pain.

"We need you to open a door and get us home safely!" her mom said. "Thargon knows we're here. There's no way to rescue Esmerelda now."

"I won't do that. Aunt Esme needs us. If we leave now, we won't get another chance."

"What are you thinking then, Kate?" Claraseve asked.

"We get to the bridge. Most of Thargon's men will be searching for us, which will leave the bridge less armed. We'll have the element of surprise since they'll never expect us to waltz up to Thargon."

"Where have I heard that before?" her mom snorted. "Can't you just open a door to the bridge and get us there faster?"

"I'm exhausted from keeping the door open. I need some time to recover and since there's no spa for me to relax in, I thought we should try to get to the bridge the old-fashioned way." Kate snapped.

"According to the schematics, there's a garbage holding tank about five hundred meters to the right. We can get inside and should be able to scale the chute to the first level where the bridge is located." Bethtizmo pointed.

"The schematics were wrong about the cells," her mom pointed out.

"We don't have much of a choice. The only other option is to try to take the lifts to the bridge but those are probably guarded," Bethtizmo replied with a tight smile.

"He's right, Mom."

"I knew this was going to be a bad day when I woke up," her mom muttered.

They sprinted the five hundred meters to the door, which Bethtizmo grabbed and tugged open. They all gagged at the smells coming from the depths.

"Oh my God, are you sure this is the only way?" Maggie asked, holding her nose as she retched.

"It's the safest way," Bethtizmo said. "Kate wanted a way to the bridge, this is a way to the bridge. After you."

One by one they crawled through the opening and jumped down into the main garbage tank, sinking knee-deep into muck. They waded into the middle of the chamber and looked up at the large cylindrical chute above their heads.

"How do we get up there?"

"You'll have to stand on my shoulders and pull yourselves up. When the last one has gone up, reach down and pull me up," Bethtizmo said.

"Easier said than done. What if you drop me?" her mom demanded. "Who knows what's in this crap. In fact, it smells WORSE than crap."

"You'll just have to trust me," Bethtizmo said through clenched teeth.

"Mom, you knew this wasn't going to be easy, but you chose to come. Keep going."

"I know. I just—the stench burns."

"Just go! The sooner we get up the sooner we get out of it." Kate threw her hands up and her mom nodded.

One by one they were hoisted up until only Bethtizmo remained. Kate wrapped her legs tightly around the rungs and held Claraseve's legs as she reached down and pulled him up and they began the long climb up.

"Oh my god, how much garbage do they make a day?" Maggie yelled as more noxious material was dumped from above and splashed them with thick brown ooze.

The sound of retching came from below.

"Are you OK?" Kate called down.

"I'm going to burn these clothes and take a weeklong bath when we get back," her mom replied.

"Claraseve?"

"I'm fine."

"We should be getting close. WATCH OUT!" Bethtizmo shouted. A large chunk of twisted metal hurtled down the chute towards them at a sickening speed. They were trapped. It would take too long to go back down and there were no exits within sight. Everyone braced for impact.

"Kate!" her mom screamed as Kate—eyes closed and bathed in the crystal's light—floated up to meet the mass of tangled metal. Light shot from her chest as her body was flung back and froze the metal in its path. The metal grew red hot and melted midair as it swirled above their heads, until it vaporized and nothing was left. Everyone sat motionless and stared at Kate until her eyes opened and she dropped. Claraseve lunged, legs wrapped around the ladder rung, and caught her before she plunged down the chute.

"Well, that was interesting," Bethtizmo said. "Useful trick. You didn't tell us you could vaporize things."

Kate's chest heaved with the exertion and her limbs shook. "I didn't know I could. It felt like the necklace took over, almost like it knew it would take too long to show me what to do. Just give me a minute and then we can go on."

"Take all the time you need. It's not like we don't have an entire ship searching for us right now," Bethtizmo said sarcastically.

Kate glared at Bethtizmo. "You can be an ass, you know that?"

"Yes, but an alive ass. Now let's keep going."

"You better have good news for me about the third realm, Kr'll." Thargon faced his third in command as he strode in and shook black dust off his cloak.

"It went well. We killed the rebellion hiding on the planet and took the planet's ironium. It should be enough," Kr'll replied.

Thargon eyed Kr'll from his seat. "How long will it take to make?"

"Shreg says it'll take a few weeks now that he has all the components."

Thargon clenched his fist and glared at Kr'll. "Tell him he has one week."

"I'll relay the message." Kr'll bowed his head at Thargon. He straightened and pointed to Esmerelda's limp body next to Thargon. "Is that one dead?"

"Not yet."

"Aren't you afraid it'll—"

"What? Run off? It doesn't have the strength, and I have my men." Thargon gestured towards the armed men scattered around the bridge.

"Where are the rest of your men?" Kr'll remarked as his eyes narrowed.

"Busy at the moment," Thargon said.

Kr'll raised an eyebrow, dropped into an empty seat, and eyed Esmerelda's crumpled body. "If you're not careful you'll break it, Thargon. I'm assuming it still hasn't given you any answers?"

"No," Thargon spat out, "but it will. Eventually they always tell me what I want to know."

"There are faster ways, you know," Kr'll said.

"I know what I'm doing. She's the only one with the information and if she dies…" Thargon turned and paced the deck.

Kr'll looked towards Nim huddled against the wall. "If you're not careful you'll kill them both. Has it made anything useful lately?"

"You're starting to irritate me, Kr'll. Be careful with your words," Thargon said slowly.

"That one is stalling, Thargon. Maybe if she made a device capable of opening doors longer than a few minutes, you'd still have your fingers—"

Kr'll's words were cut off as Thargon's remaining fingers closed around his throat. Kr'll struggled to breathe and clawed at Thargon's hands as Thargon brought Kr'll's face closer until it was inches from his.

"Don't think I haven't noticed you become a little too familiar. This is my ship, not yours. I'm the one in charge, not you. It will never be you and do you know why? Because you're weaker. I'll always be stronger and smarter than you. So, know your place. Do we understand each other?"

Kr'll gurgled, unable to speak as a string of drool dribbled down his chin.

"I'm glad we've had this talk." Thargon dropped Kr'll on the floor where he lay, gasping.

Thargon turned and stared out at the expanse of space on the screens before him.

One of his men approached. "Your supremeness, they've searched the lower levels and there's no sign of them."

"Tell them if they don't find the intruders, things will become very unpleasant for them. I'll start by cutting off limbs. Or I can leave them on Drog, their choice."

"But we need the men—"

"And I need the intruders found."

"Yes, my lord."

Kate and the others pulled themselves out of the garbage chute one by one and crouched into a small alcove tucked away from the main hall.

"How are we going to sneak onto the bridge smelling like this?" Maggie whispered as she held her foul-smelling shirt away from her body and turned her head.

"We don't," Claraseve replied. "We're going to use the element of surprise. Kate, are you strong enough now?"

Kate nodded.

Bethtizmo jerked his head toward the direction of the bridge. "There could be anywhere between fifteen to twenty of Thargon's men on the bridge, less if he's sent some off to look for us. I suggest we split up, flank the sides, and take cover when we get through. With luck we can take out most of his men before they realize we're in."

"I'll open the door—"

"Won't that give us away?" Maggie questioned. "It is a bit noisy, Kate."

"There are other ways, Maggie," Kate replied with a tight smile.

"After Kate opens the door, Bethtizmo and Janice go left. Maggie and I will go right. Bethtizmo and I can take out quite a few of them—"

"I'm a good shot too," her mom said.

"I'm sure you are, Janice. Just try not to shoot your sister. Maggie, remember to aim for the chest and squeeze the trigger. You got this. Kate, you—"

"Don't worry about me. I know what to do," Kate replied, shoulders set.

Claraseve looked at Kate hard. "OK. The bridge is down that corridor. Hopefully we won't run into anyone on the way, but if we do, leave them to Bethtizmo or me. Ready? Let's go."

Bethtizmo led the way as they darted down the corridor. They kept to the sides where the light didn't fully penetrate and stopped just outside the bridge doors.

Kate's heart slammed against her chest at the thought of how close they were. She focused on the crystal as she opened her mind and showed it what she wanted. The crystal responded and bathed her in its glow as power surged through her body. She reached out her hand and placed her palm on the control panel by the door. Energy surged through her body and into the panel as smoke poured out and the doors opened. Weapons drawn, they charged in. Four bodies fell as Claraseve and the others opened fire and dove for cover before Thargon's men registered what happened and returned fire.

"I want them alive! I WANT THEM ALIVE!" Thargon bellowed over the din.

"Kate, whatever you're going to do, I suggest you do it now!" Claraseve hollered as small cylinders shot over their heads and landed behind them. Smoke seeped out, and everyone but Kate began to cough from the noxious fumes. They covered their mouths with their shirts as the smoke burned their lungs and eyes. Thargon's men, who didn't appear affected by the smoke as it filled the bridge, took advantage. Crouched down they approached, cautiously.

"ALIVE, YOU IDIOTS!" Thargon roared. He grabbed one of his men who had shot blindly into smoke, snapped his arm in two, and dropped him onto the floor.

Kate rose up, an ethereal being bathed in the glow of the crystal, and calmly walked towards Thargon's men. Her hands dipped and wove in the air and chants flowed off her tongue as easily as a child's nursery rhyme. The smoke thinned but still clung to the floor.

"Bachma Lekma Soren! Bachma Lekma Soren Dippa Mora LIEN!"

Thargon's men grabbed at her but were thrown across the ship when their hands encountered the glow surrounding Kate. She felt power surge through her as the crystal amplified it. She had never felt so alive or in tune with who she was. She stepped into her power. She was the last Harrikan and the key to the universe. The crystal bathed her in love and rejoiced, as the voices rose in a crescendo and sang its praises.

"KATE," her mom screamed as one of Thargon's men leapt in front of her and fired a fatal shot.

Shock registered on its face as Kate absorbed the energy, unfazed. It fired again and again, yet each time Kate absorbed the weapon's energy as her glow burned brighter, until it dropped its weapon and bolted out the main door. She continued to chant and walked on until she stopped a few feet from Thargon's silhouette.

"Surrender or she dies, descendant of Jones," Thargon said as he casually grabbed Esmerelda's limp form and held her above his head.

Kate responded by chanting louder as a hole opened up behind Thargon. Wind filled the bridge and cleared out the rest of the gas. The others struggled to their feet and gathered behind Kate, weapons trained on both Thargon and Kr'll.

Thargon glanced behind him and looked at Kate with a calculated look.

"You opened the doors. How is that possible? No matter. It appears I have the wrong Jones. You are going to be very useful to me. Very useful indeed."

"Let Esmerelda go," Kate shouted above the din as she stood her ground.

"Ahh, but I won't. You see, I'm stronger so I will win. Your weapons, a mere nuisance, cannot hurt me, so I will win. Even if all your puny selves rush me, you cannot hope to push me through, and I will win. In every scenario I am stronger, smarter, more cunning, and I will win. So, the outcome is inevitable: I . . . will . . . win . . ." Thargon shook Esmerelda's body with each word.

"Who said anything about pushing you, Thargon?" Kate tilted her head and smiled.

Thargon looked down as a long black tentacle reached from the depths of the blackness and eagerly searched for flesh. It reached Thargon's ankle, wound around and jerked him off his feet as it sliced through his skin. He dropped Esmerelda, drew his gun and shot the tentacle, but another quickly replaced it, reaching from the dark.

Thargon scrambled backwards, but other tentacles slithered across the floor towards him. They smelled the smeared blood Thargon left on the floor, quivered, and honed in on Thargon yet again. Each tentacle crept with stealth and purpose towards its prey. Thargon shot as the tentacles reached for him, but there were too many and they were hungry. Soon they overwhelmed Thargon and slowly pulled him into the abyss as his hands searched for anything to grab onto.

"Kr'll, help me!"

"I'm sorry, my Liege, I don't think I'm strong enough to help."

In desperation Thargon grabbed Esmerelda's foot as Kate and her mom lunged for her.

"Stop this or she shares the same fate!"

Seconds later he looked in surprise at his spurting stump where his arm used to be as Esmerelda broke free. He looked at Janice's grim face as she threw down her weapon and he was whisked away into the dark dimension.

Kate slammed the door shut with a bang and sank next to her mom and aunt. Her mom moved Esme's hair out of her face gently. Esmerelda opened her eyes and looked into her sister's as the two hugged each other.

"Well, this has been interesting," Kr'll replied.

"Stay where you are," Claraseve and Bethtizmo said in unison, weapons trained on him.

Kr'll eyed Claraseve. "I seem to remember you from Deprama. Fear not, I have no plans for you or that creature. I'm going to have my hands full taking over Thargon's empire."

"So, you're just going to let us leave?" Claraseve asked.

"If you leave, you won't tell anyone what happened, which works in my favor."

"Then you wouldn't mind backing up and tossing your weapon over here," Claraseve instructed.

Kr'll tossed his weapon and backed away as the others moved to help Esmeralda.

"Kate, I'd really like to get home," Esmerelda whispered.

"Then let's go home."

"Not without me," a voice spoke up. They looked as a small figure sat up and shook off the debris. "Nim!" Bethtizmo cried. He strode over to her and caught her as she tripped on her shackles. He scooped her up and brought her over to the growing group. "Quick girl, make the door. I don't want to spend another second on this hellhole."

Kate's hands moved and flowed as she chanted with an air of confidence.

"Lemes Cron Deseble. Lemes Cron Deseble. Lemes Cron Deseble."

"One day, you are going to have to show me how you do that," Kr'll murmured.

"Not if I can help it," Kate replied as she followed the others through the door, home.

26) The Aftermath

"A Harrikan? Well, I would say I'm surprised but I'm not. I knew the day I showed you the necklace," Aunt Esme said from her bed. It had only been a day since the rescue, and she was still weak. "And the other shards of Akashte? What about those?"

Kate hesitated for a split second before divulging her plans. "I'm going to find them. I can hear them, faintly, out there." Kate gazed out the window towards the stars hidden by the light of day. "I'm not sure what happens when we get all the pieces, but I'll figure that out."

"*We'll* figure that out," her aunt stated firmly. "You don't think I'm going to let you go alone and have all the adventures, do you? Besides, there are things I need to teach you about traveling, and there's no one else to show you. Unless you want to ask your mom."

Kate grinned at her aunt. "That's ok, I think I'll pass. I was going to ask anyway when you were feeling better."

"Speaking of your mom, where is she?"

"Spending the day with Dad. She has a lot of explaining to do, but she said she'd be back. Something about you guys needing to talk about a lot of things."

Aunt Esme grabbed Kate's hand and squeezed, "And I hear you're responsible for that too. Thank you. I thought I lost my sister years ago. Ah, I know it's going to take time but the fact that she even wants to work on our relationship is amazing." Her aunt's eyes slowly closed, and Kate crept out of the room. Aunt Esme needed her rest and Kate had things to do.

"I thought I'd find you here. The others are waiting," Maggie said as she approached Kate. Kate put her brush down, smiled, and felt the dry paint crackle on her cheek. It had been over a week since they'd been home, and Kate had sought solace in her art and the nook while Aunt Esme and Nim regained their strength. Eyes so like her own stared back from the canvas.

"Who is that? She looks like you, only older," Maggie said as she examined the woman.

"She's my ancestor. The first one to come through," Kate replied.

"I still can't believe it," Maggie said. Kate had filled her in on her vision soon after they had gotten back. "My best friend, a *Harrikan*, with a piece of a god for a necklace."

Kate shook her head at her friend and laughed. "It's not really like that."

"No? OK, have it your way." Maggie looked her friend over. "I told you this house was good for you. You glow."

"I suppose I do." Kate grabbed a towel and scrubbed at her cheek. She knew Maggie was right: this house was good for her. She smiled at her friend.

"Are you sure you want to do this?" Maggie's fingers squeezed her shoulder.

Kate rubbed the crystal necklace and felt a glow of love in response. "I'm sure. Aunt Esme and I need to go find the other shards of Akashte. They're out there." Kate smiled at her best friend. "I wish you'd reconsider. I'm going to miss you."

"I'm going to miss you too, but you and your aunt have got this. I would just get in the way. Ahp," Maggie held up her hand, "I know my limitations and out there, I'm not that helpful. I saw how you handled things on Thargon's ship, and you don't need me. Besides, I have a life and a career here."

"You have an amazing career. And I'll visit when I can and get Nim to work on a way to communicate so we can keep in touch." Kate's eyes welled with tears, and she brushed them away. "Anyway, the offer stands if you ever change your mind."

Maggie hugged her and pulled away as they both wiped away more tears. They walked into the parlor where everyone had gathered. Kate looked over at her aunt who already looked healthier and Nim, well, Nim was Nim. She took a seat between her mom and aunt as Nim began:

"You know the story up to the point where the grifters invaded my home. They're a nasty lot but I'm tough and old and not much use to them so they sold me off. They had no idea I was a Peradite, otherwise they never would have sold me off and used me for their own twisted needs." Nim shuddered before continuing. "I was sold a handful of times because of my temperament, if you can believe that. One idjit tried to put me in the kitchen but people started dying mysteriously. I got wind that they planned to execute me, but I made a show about my 'abilities.' They were a superstitious lot, so I made the walls ooze red slime. As far as I'm aware they're still oozing. They sold me off pretty quickly after that and seemed to be afraid of me.

"Rightfully so," Bethtizmo muttered.

Nim cackled at Bethtizmo and continued.

"The last place I was at was a nasty outer planet, and I had just tricked my owner into freeing me when Thargon found me. I don't know how he knew I was a Peradite, but he knew. He bought me off that scumbag cheat after he had already agreed to free me. I may have to pay him a visit when this is all over," Nim murmured before she continued. "Thargon brought me on board his ship and started me working on ways to create doors between dimensions."

"Did he know you already knew how?" Bethtizmo asked.

"Just when I thought you weren't so stupid. Of course, he didn't know. Otherwise, we'd be dead." Nim shook her head at Bethtizmo.

"Then why didn't you create one and use it to escape?" he scoffed back at her.

"I overheard them talking one night about Esmerelda's pitiful attempt to rescue me. They brought her on board the next day. I couldn't leave after she tried to save me. I knew if I left it would be worse for her. I played it off like I needed materials that were extremely difficult to get. Once he got the materials, I tried stalling by making doors that only stayed open for a few seconds."

"That must have infuriated him." Kate smirked.

"It did but there was nothing he could do about it. He couldn't prove I was sabotaging his plans and he needed me. Unfortunately, I got tired and sloppy. That's when he came through the door the first time and you sent him packing with flower pollen and a staff."

"You played a very dangerous game, Nim," Bethtizmo said.

"It was more dangerous for him, apparently. Look what you did to him. Turned him into tentacle food. How'd you do that anyway?" Nim asked Kate.

"I remembered a dimension my mom told me about. We couldn't defeat him in this dimension right now and there weren't many other dimensions I knew of capable of containing him. Seemed like the perfect solution."

"Smart girl. Like your aunt. Anyway, that's when you lot showed up and things got interesting, and you saved us. The rest you know."

Everyone looked towards Esmerelda.

"I'm afraid it's rather a short story. I had gotten wind that Thargon had a Peradite. I couldn't be sure it was Nim but knew what it meant. He was trying to find a way to Trilesk. I spent months gathering information on where they were being held, even going as far as to infiltrate Deprama to scour their computers for their location."

"Why didn't you just ask another Peradite to make you something like Nim did?" Kate's face scrunched in confusion.

"They couldn't do it. Nim's one of the best."

Bethtizmo scoffed and Nim glared at him.

"Scoff all you want, Bethtizmo, but Nim is one of the greatest inventors of Peradite history. The others wouldn't even attempt to try what she did. They said it was too unstable and the hole could grow and swallow entire galaxies."

Bethtizmo gulped, "Is that possible, Nim?"

"Anything's a possibility," she replied slyly.

Bethtizmo suddenly looked very uncomfortable.

"Thargon unexpectedly came back to Deprama and recognized me, even years later. He knew I helped get Miswala out and would know where to find them. He's been searching for years, obsessing over their energy and the weapons it could make. He once said he wanted to wage wars with the gods."

"How do you even find gods to wage wars with?" Claraseve asked.

"I don't know. I never asked. Thargon was driven to prove he was unstoppable and defeated everything he came across. Well, until you guys came along."

"He never defeated you either, Esme. You stood against him day after day. It must have been horrific," her mom replied softly.

"The horrific part was when he actually opened the door and came through. Thargon had guards over me, and I didn't have the strength to fight them and or come through. I just sat and watched as Thargon chased after you, knowing that even if he caught you, I wouldn't give him what he wanted. After you sent him flying back through the door, he was livid. He couldn't stand the thought that he was thwarted by a mere girl, a couple of mice, and flowers, or that it was witnessed by his best men. He killed them all just to make sure no one questioned his prowess as a leader. The rest, you know." Esme paused to gather her thoughts before she continued. "Thank you for saving me, saving us. You all risked your lives to bring us back, and I will forever be grateful to you."

"Ditto what she said. Don't expect any more emotional crap from me either." Nim glared at everyone, but no one was fooled.

"What now?" Kate asked the others after a few moments of silence had passed.

"Claraseve and I have to go back to our dimensions. I'm still looking for Sol and we'll need to keep an eye on Kr'll. I don't think we've heard the last of him."

Nim spoke up from her chair, "I'm going with Bethtizmo and Claraseve. It's the best use of my abilities."

"Are you sure you can handle being around me?" Bethtizmo asked.

"I've grown fond of you, and you need someone clever on board," Nim cackled.

"I—"

Clarazeve shook her head at him. "Let it go," she replied softly.

Bethtizmo changed the subject. "We heard you're going after the other shards, Kate. You know if you happen to swing by our dimension, we'll be happy to help. Besides, I'd like to study your necklace a bit more."

"When are you and Esmerelda leaving?" Mrs. B asked with a slight frown.

Kate smiled at her. "Don't worry. We're giving Aunt Esme time to recover. It won't be for at least a month. Besides, there's a lot I have to learn before we make our first trip. And it'll give me, mom and Aunt Esme time to work on things."

"We have a lot to work through. I can admit when I'm wrong,

and apparently, I've been wrong about a lot," her mom said.

"I would have said that was impossible not that long ago," Maggie said and shook her head in disbelief.

"You know, Maggie, I have a saying about the impossible," Esmerelda piped up as everyone groaned.

THE END

From the Author

Thank you, dear readers! I hope you enjoyed *The Door to Trilesk* as much as I enjoyed writing it (minus the tears, I did not enjoy the tears). This book has gone through so many rounds of edits and re-writes all with the aim to produce the best possible version for you, the reader. The idea for this book came to me when I bought my first home. I was pondering how to decorate it with my style, when an image of a woman popped into my head. I decided I wanted my home to look like a dimensional traveler lived there with all the unique bits from her travels. Thus, Esmerelda Jones was born. I can't wait to discover what other adventures await her and Kate and the others. If you love this book, there are several ways to help an indie author out.

What can you do?

- Leave an honest review from the site you bought this book from or go on Goodreads.
- Tell a friend.
- Post on social media and tag me @shannonhollyauthor. I love to see your posts!

- Sign up for my author newsletter for updates on new releases. I send one out twice a month www.shannonholly.com/newsletter
- Follow me on social media, BookBub, Goodreads or Amazon.

Acknowledgements

I'd like to thank my editors PJ Hoover and Molly Spain, as well as my last-minute editor, Christine Holly. You all rock and were amazing. The story is so much richer than before, and I know all my commas are where they should be. It took a team effort and this team rocked! This book wouldn't be what it is today without you guys.

Thank you to Polgarus Studio for writing the book blurb and formatting it. I could not be happier with the results and with a name from my favorite childhood book series, I knew I couldn't go wrong.

Thank you to my mom, Linda Holly, and best friend, Kiersten Pasciak, for their endless support and for reading each endless re-write with enthusiasm. You two cheered me on from the beginning and pushed me through the doubts. You listened to all the book title names, plot point ideas, changes, character developments, everything, and gave me freedom to talk as much as I wanted without being judged. You two are amazing and I love you both.

Thank you to my kids, Jared and Katie Kuharik, for giving me time, space and understanding. Over three years I was holed up in my room, and then my office. I wrote before work when I worked second shifts and then in the mornings when I switched to weekends. You two never complained about my absence or when dinner was late and were always understanding. I love you both immensely.

Thank you to my dad, Charles Holly. You let me ramble on and on about all the business stuff I was learning, even if you didn't understand what I was talking about. You are outstanding and I love you. I can always count on you to be my rock.

Thank you to my stepdad, Rick Gillespie, for letting me talk shop without getting tired of hearing about it. Even though it's different than the original, I hope you like it. I love you and hope to read your book one day.

Thank you to all my beta readers for taking the time to read the book in its raw form and offering feedback.

Thank you to everyone who asked about it during the process, supported me and cheered me on. I appreciate you all more than you can know.

About the Author

Shannon is a GenX author who grew up feral, reading the likes of Eddings, CS Lewis, McCaffrey, and watching Star Trek, Star Wars and Battlestar Galactica. She's devoted to giving her fans the same sense of wonder and excitement she grew up with. She loves to hear from her fans so drop her line through her website www.shannonholly.com or through social media.